FI

Donut Mystery #12

From *New York Times* Bestselling Author Jessica Beck

SWEET SUSPECTS

To Emily!

Other Books by Jessica Beck

The Donut Shop Mysteries

Glazed Murder
Fatally Frosted
Sinister Sprinkles
Evil Éclairs
Tragic Toppings
Killer Crullers
Drop Dead Chocolate
Powdered Peril
Illegally Iced
Deadly Donuts
Assault and Batter
Sweet Suspects

The Classic Diner Mysteries

A Chili Death
A Deadly Beef
A Killer Cake
A Baked Ham
A Bad Egg
A Real Pickle

The Ghost Cat Cozy Mysteries

Ghost Cat: Midnight Paws
Ghost Cat 2: Bid for Midnight

"If one donut is good, then two must be even better!"
Sad to admit it, but this one's from the author!

Chapter 1

"Don't I know you?" the drunken man wearing three different plastic leis asked as he cornered me in the high school gymnasium. Though the place was decorated with crepe paper and streamers for our combined high school reunions, there was no hiding the normal utilitarian function of the space. There wasn't enough bunting in the world to disguise that. Keeping with the Hawaiian luau theme, a pair of decorative spears held up a colorful banner over the DJ that said *Welcome Back, ASHS Students*. Some genius had decided to host three class reunions at the same time, and I'd reluctantly agreed to go, even though my boyfriend, State Police Inspector Jake Bishop, was on the Outer Banks up to his hips in another murder. Grace Gauge, my best friend since childhood, had convinced me that it would be fun, but so far, it had taken all that I had not to run out of the building as though it were on fire.

"Of course you know me," I said. "Billy Briscoe, we were in most of the same classes all through high school. It's me, Suzanne Hart."

"Sweet little Suzie Q," he said, slurring a nickname that I would never answer to. "You look great," he added as he leaned in. His clothes were so heavy with the smell of alcohol that I was amazed he could even still stand.

"You're drunk," I said, lacking any sympathy for the balding man with a middle-age spread that I had once considered cute. Wow, what a difference a few years made.

"That I am," he said with a grin. "You wanna sneak away with me into the shadows for a minute or two?"

"Not even the least little bit," I said as I spotted Grace walking toward us.

"Come on. You know you wanna," he said as he added an overstated wink.

Grace joined us, smiling. "There you are, Billy. Did you know that Sandy Link has been looking all over the gym for you?"

That got his attention. Sandy had been the head cheerleader once upon a time, and she'd kept up her appearance to the point where it wouldn't have surprised me if she'd shown up in her old uniform. It clearly would still fit. "Sandy?" he asked as he started scanning the room. "Where is she?"

"The last time that I saw her, she was standing over by the men's restroom," Grace said.

Billy started off, abandoning me without a second thought, much to my pleasure. "Grace, what would *Sandy* want with *him*?"

"She doesn't, as far as I know, but you looked as though you'd had enough of Billy."

"Wow, are you taking a chance. Do you remember how bad a temper Billy has? In the old days, he'd go crazy over a lot less."

"I'm willing to bet that he won't remember *any* of our conversation by morning," Grace said.

"Remind me again, Grace. *Why* did we come here?" I asked as I glanced at the caged clock high on the wall. "You said that this would be fun, remember?"

"It is," Grace said with a good-natured smile. "You just need to have the right frame of mind, Suzanne."

"Well, I'm giving it five more minutes, and then I'm taking off. I have to get up early tomorrow to make donuts, remember?"

"I'm not about to forget that," she said as a handsome fellow interrupted us.

"Grace? Is that you?" There was a definite gleam in his eyes as he studied her, and Grace returned every ounce of it.

"Tom Hancock, as I live and breathe. How are you?"

"Truth be told, I'm single again," Tom said. "I saw you looking around the gym a minute ago, and if you tell me that you were trying to find me, you'll make my day."

Grace laughed, and I smiled as well. She and Tom had been high school sweethearts, but they'd chosen different colleges. They'd drifted apart over the years, but it was good seeing them together again.

"You are too charming for your own good," Grace said, and then she turned to me. "You remember Suzanne, don't you?"

"Of course I do. It's great to see you again, Suzanne," Tom said, turning those dazzling blue eyes on me. He was even better looking than he had been in high school, and I found myself fighting back an unexpected giggle. I reminded myself that I had a very significant other in my life as I tried to suppress my girlish laugh.

"It's really nice to see you, too," I said.

He looked around the crowded gym. "Where's Max? Are you two still together?"

It was my turn to laugh now. "Not for a long time. I divorced him quite awhile ago."

"I'm sorry to hear that," Tom said.

"I'm not," I replied with a smile. "After our marriage broke up, I met someone *much* better than Max."

"Is he here with you tonight?" Tom asked as he looked around yet again. "I'd love to meet him."

"No, he's away working," I said.

"More's the pity," Tom answered, and then he looked back at Grace. "I've been afraid to ask you this, but I can't stand the suspense one second longer. Is there someone special in your life, Grace?"

"No, not at the moment," Grace said.

"Wow, I'm really sorry to hear that," Tom answered with a huge grin on his face.

"Try to contain yourself. I can tell that you're all broken up by the news," she replied.

Just then, the DJ played a song from our school days, and Tom bowed deeply to Grace. "May I have this dance?"

"You may," Grace said before she turned to me. "Suzanne, you don't mind, do you?"

"Not at all. You kids have fun," I said.

"Thanks," Grace replied, and Tom took her hand and led her out onto the dance floor. They still looked good together, and it made me smile seeing Grace so happy. Maybe Tom would stick around after the reunion. My best friend *deserved* someone good in her life. I saw Gary Thorpe standing to one side, a classmate who now owned a camera shop in town. He was taking video of the entire affair, though for the life of me, I couldn't imagine why anyone would care.

I was still watching Grace and Tom dance when an angry man nearly plowed into me where I stood on the sidelines. "Always the watcher, never the achiever, right, Hart?" Zane Dunbar asked with a frown. He'd been a bully all through school, and from the way he was acting at the moment, it was pretty clear that he hadn't changed all that much over the years.

The difference now was that I didn't have to put up with him. "Go away, Zane. Nobody cares about what you think anymore."

"That's just too bad," he said. "I'm not going anywhere, and I'd like to see somebody try to throw me out."

A mousy-looking woman approached us tentatively, and I was surprised to see that it was Janet Yeager. She'd been so soft spoken through school that she'd barely made an impression on most folks. Janet looked at the man in front of me and said, "Zane, I think that you've had enough to drink."

He looked at her with raw anger. "You don't tell me what to do, Janet. If you don't like it, go back to the hotel."

I couldn't help myself as I blurted out, "You two are *together*?"

"We're married, yes," Janet said almost apologetically.

"For now," Zane said as he scanned the dance floor. "There he is. I'm going to get even with that jerk if it's the last thing I do."

"Don't do anything you'll regret," Janet pleaded, but Zane was already off.

"He's usually not like this," Janet said to me. "I wish he wouldn't drink so much. He's already had an argument with Mr. Davidson and Helen Marston, and now this."

"I'm so sorry," I said, for more reasons that I chose not to list, most of all that I was sorry that she'd decided to marry Zane in the first place.

To my dismay, Zane headed straight for Tom. "There you are," he said loudly. "Did you think you could hide from me all night?"

"Zane, you're drunk," Tom said, barely interrupting his dance with Grace.

"Yeah, that might be true, but you're a liar and a cheat. I want my money back," Zane pressed.

"Everybody lost their shirts on that deal. There's no money left to give."

"You mark my words," Zane said as he stuck a meaty finger in Tom's chest, stopping their dance. "I'll get it back one way or the other."

Tom knocked the finger away, causing Zane to stumble a little. "Don't push me, Zane," he said.

"You just wait," Zane answered. He leaned toward Grace and whispered something in her ear, something that made her face go suddenly pale.

As she stumbled back away from him, Tom moved in. "Leave her out of this, Zane."

"Try and stop me," Zane snapped. He started to take a swing at Tom, but the man neatly sidestepped the punch and Zane went sprawling out onto the floor. Janet raced to help him, but when she got there, he knocked her hand away. "Leave me alone, woman. I don't need your help," he said.

Just then, Officer Grant approached. He was one of Chief Martin's best cops, and a friend of mine as well, not on duty but attending the reunion on his free time. Officer Grant loved donuts, and he wasn't afraid of being tagged with any of the jokes about cops and donuts. He reached down and grabbed Zane's arm in one swift motion. "Come on. Let's get you some fresh air."

"Get your hands off me," Zane snapped as he tried to free himself, but the police officer was too strong for him.

"Outside right now," Officer Grant said in a no-nonsense manner as he deftly walked Zane out of the gym without making too much of a scene.

I hurried over to Janet. "Are you okay?"

"I'm fine," she said, clearly looking embarrassed by the entire confrontation that had just occurred. "I'd better go see how Zane is doing."

"You might want to give him a little time to cool off first," I said.

"I wish I could, but I can't. Bye, Suzanne."

"Bye, Janet," I said as she headed outside. It wasn't my job to stop her, but I still didn't like the thought of her going outside while her husband was in such a mood. Her husband. It was still nearly impossible for me to believe, but then again, I was sure that a few folks had been surprised when I'd ended up with Max.

Grace and Tom were still dancing, but they were talking earnestly now as well. After the song ended, Grace quickly walked over to me, but Tom stayed right where he was, staring after her.

"What just happened?" I asked Grace. "What did Zane say to you, Grace?"

"It's too complicated to go into right now," she said. "Are you ready to leave?"

I looked over at Tom, who appeared to be in shock by her sudden dismissal. "Are you sure that you want to go?"

"I'm positive," she said.

There was no debate in her voice. "Let's go, then."

I wasn't sure where Zane, Officer Grant, and Janet had gone, but they weren't in the parking lot when we left the building. It had been a chilly evening, but we'd walked over to the school together from my house, and as we headed back down Springs Drive, I told Grace, "I won't push you about what just happened, but remember, I'm here if you need me."

"I know. Let's just not talk right now, okay?"

"That's fine with me," I said as we started walking back home in silence. There are a great many kinds of silences in our lives, from awkward moments on first dates to uncomfortable situations where we just don't know what to say. Though Grace was clearly troubled by what Zane had said to her earlier, this wasn't one of those uncomfortable moments. We'd been friends long enough to be able to share quiet moments comfortably, secure in the depth of our relationship. We walked past the bank, the newspaper office, and then city hall. ReNEWed, Gabby Williams's shop, was just down from that, and then we were in front of Donut Hearts. It was my very own place, a business I'd bought with my divorce settlement, and now it was as much my home as the cottage that I shared with my mother. Grace and I walked across the long-abandoned railroad tracks, and I thought yet again of my late friend, James Settle. He'd been killed in the park across the street from where we now walked, a blacksmith struck down in senseless death, and I found myself missing him yet again. He'd deeded the rights to the tracks to me, and I promised myself that I'd hold onto them forever.

Soon enough we were at Grace's place, and I walked with her up the steps of her front porch.

"If you don't feel like being alone, you're welcome to come home with me," I said. "Momma's out with Chief Martin, but I'm sure we can find *something* decadent in the fridge."

"If it's all the same to you, I think I'll just stay here," she said.

"I understand, but call me anytime, okay? I'm always available to you."

"Thanks," Grace said, and as she reached out to touch my shoulder lightly, I saw that her hand was shaking a little. What had Zane said that had made such an impact on her? She'd most likely tell me eventually, but I wasn't about to press her at the moment. There would be time enough later.

Or so I thought.

As I'd predicted, Momma was gone when I got home, and with Jake busy working across the state, I decided to take a long hot shower and get ready for bed. Sleep came quickly, and when my alarm clock rang six hours later, I felt ready to tackle a brand-new day. After getting dressed and tiptoeing downstairs, I grabbed a bagel on my way out the door and did my best not to wake Momma. Our schedules were completely different, and it was a rare day when she was awake in the morning as I left for work.

I drove the short distance between my place and my business on Springs Drive in the quiet of the night, savoring the silence and the sheer solitude of the darkness.

As I pulled in to park in front of the donut shop, my headlights caught someone, most likely a man, judging by his silhouette, sitting slumped forward on a bench in the park across from my shop.

That was odd. There appeared to be a long taper beside him on the bench.

He hadn't moved when my lights hit him. Could he be asleep? I parked out of the way of any potential traffic that might come down the road and I got out of the Jeep, my heart in my throat as I walked toward him.

"Hello? Excuse me. Are you okay?" I called out before I could get a good look at him.

There was no response, and as I got a few steps closer, I could see why.

Someone had stabbed the man in the chest with one of the spears I'd seen at the reunion just a few short hours ago. I hadn't been able to make out the weapon earlier because of the poor light, but that wasn't the most disturbing thing about the crime scene.

It was someone I knew.

When I realized that Zane Dunbar was the murder victim, I realized that it was time to call the police, no matter what the ramifications of that conversation might mean to my friends and me.

Chapter 2

"Chief Martin here," the police chief said as he answered the phone at the police station.

"What are you doing up at this hour?" I asked. I knew that the chief rarely worked nights, preferring to be off when my mother was available for a date. He'd worked hard to woo her, and I knew that the man never passed up the chance to be with her.

"Got a bit of insomnia so I thought I'd come on in and make good use of it," he admitted. "What's going on, Suzanne?"

"I hate to tell you this, but I just found a dead body near the donut shop," I said.

After a moment's pause, he said, "Are you serious?"

"I *wish* I were kidding, but unfortunately, I'm not," I said, still shaking a little from just discovering Zane's body. I didn't think that I'd *ever* get used to stumbling across someone who had just been murdered. As a matter of fact, I hoped that I *never* did. No matter who the victim might be, no matter how awful a person they seemed, nobody deserved that kind of end, and it never failed to shake me to my core. "It's Zane Dunbar, and it appears that someone stabbed him in the chest with one of those ceremonial spears they used during the reunion last night. As close as I could tell, someone pinned him to the bench with it, and before you ask, I'm pretty sure that he's dead. He was cold to the touch, anyway." I shivered again as I remembered checking for a pulse and not finding even the slightest flutter of motion under my fingertips.

"I'm on my way. I don't have to tell you not to touch anything, do I?"

"No problem there," I said. "I'll see you soon."

Much to my relief, the chief was there in less than a

minute, screeching to a halt near my Jeep and rushing out of his car. "Hey," he said as he hurried over to Zane to check for a pulse himself. I didn't blame him. I might have easily missed something; after all, I was no trained professional.

Instead of immediately saying anything else to me, the chief got on his radio. "Call for an ambulance in front of Donut Hearts," he ordered.

"Did you find a pulse?" I asked, hoping against hope that I'd been wrong.

The chief shook his head in my direction as he continued, "After that, I need the forensics team out here on the double."

The dispatcher said something, and the chief responded, "I don't care *what* time it is. Get them *all* out of bed, and I mean right now."

Finally, Chief Martin turned to me. "Sorry you had to find him like this, Suzanne," he said, his voice suddenly softening. Since he'd been dating my mother, his attitude toward me had changed quite a bit, and if I were being honest about it, mine had toward him as well.

"I still can't believe this happened," I said.

The police chief shook his head in sadness. "It seems to occur all too often around here these days. I don't know what happened to the quiet of small town life."

"Honestly, was it ever really all *that* quiet?" I asked him.

"Probably not," he admitted as the first squad car and an ambulance both approached us. The chief looked at me and added, "We're going to be really busy over here, so if you want to go in and get started on your day, I'll come by a little later and bring you up to speed."

It wasn't a dismissal: more like an invitation that I really appreciated. "Thanks. I'll bring some coffee over as soon as it's ready."

"That would be much appreciated," he said, so I started inside. As I went in and flipped on a few lights, I headed

for the coffee urn and flipped the switch. There was a
chill in the air outside that had nothing to do with the
murder, and I knew that the chief and his staff would
appreciate something to warm them up. Ordinarily Chief
Martin wouldn't take anything free from me, but he made
an exception every now and then. As the coffee brewed,
I went about my morning trying to find some order in a
pretty chaotic beginning. It was a real comfort to me to
have something to do. Though it wouldn't eliminate the
image I still had etched into my brain of Zane Dunbar
pinned to the bench with a decorative spear, it might help
me suppress it long enough to get on with my life. Death
was no stranger to me anymore, but that didn't mean that
I had to like it.

I flipped on the switch for the fryer since the oil needed
time to heat up, and then I laid out some of the basics I'd
be needing for my first task that day, making the cake
donuts. A great many people would have been surprised
to learn that the cake donuts and the yeast ones required
two completely different processes. It was one of the
reasons that I had to get up every day at such an
inhumane hour, but I couldn't imagine not offering both
types of donuts to my customers every day.

I had a rough idea about how long the coffee would
take, and sure enough, when I walked back out front, it
was ready. Transferring it to one of my largest carafes, I
grabbed some cups as well and set up the pot to brew
another batch when I was ready for it. I wished that I had
some donuts to offer them as well, but it was a rule at
Donut Hearts that we *never* kept donuts from one day to
the next, starting off fresh every morning. It was too bad
this morning, though.

I walked across the road, surprised how quickly I'd
gotten used to the warmth of the donut shop. It was
indeed a chilly morning, and as I reached the crew of
detectives, I coughed to let the chief know that I was
back. He was deeply engrossed as he studied the murder

victim, and I wondered just what he was looking at. I had no formal training when it came to investigations, but what I did have was a willingness to ask questions, and to listen to the answers I got. I'd found over the years that it was a talent that not many folks, inside of law enforcement and not, possessed.

"Coffee's ready," I said. "Should I go ahead and pour?"

"Just put it all down over there," he said, never looking up from the body. "Thanks."

"My pleasure," I said as I did as I was told and walked back across the street. There was a bustle of activity that belied the time of morning, and I was just as glad to be heading back to a world that I was very familiar with.

"What's going on over there?" my assistant, Emma Blake, asked me as she walked into Donut Hearts a little later. I'd gotten a late start because of everything that had happened, so I still hadn't finished the batter for my cake donuts yet.

"You're going to want to go call your dad," I said, and then I brought her up to speed on what had happened earlier. I'd thought long and hard about advising Emma to phone her father, but in the end, I decided that it was the right thing to do. Ray paid a bounty for news, even to his own daughter, so at least she'd get something out of it. I could have called him myself, but I knew that Emma was saving money again, this time not for college, but for a trip to Europe, and I was glad to do anything I could to help, especially since her mother had agreed to help me out at Donut Hearts in Emma's absence.

"Are you sure?" she asked. "I don't have to."

"Call him before someone else beats you to the finder's fee," I said.

That was all it took. With a grin, she said, "Thanks. I'll be right back."

While she was gone, I put the finishing touches on the

last bit of batter and started frying the first batch of donuts. By the time Emma came back in, I was rinsing out my heavy dough dropper and preparing for another batch, this one spiced pumpkin. It was one of my best sellers, and I often toyed with the idea of keeping it on the menu year-round, but I wasn't sure they would still be special if I did that.

"I'll do that," she said.

"I've got it. Go ahead and set up the front."

"Thanks."

As she started to leave, I asked, "What did your dad say?"

"He thanked me, and then he told me to thank you," she said.

"Why thank me? I didn't do anything."

"We both beg to differ. Should I flip on the coffee pot so we can give some to the police?"

"I've already taken some over," I said, "but I could use some caffeine myself, so flip away."

"Will do, boss," she said.

As I finished the last of the cake donuts and started icing them while they were still hot, I called out to Emma, "It's safe to come back now."

"Good," she said as she walked in. "I want to get started on that first batch of dishes before we're ready to take our break."

We always took a break when the yeast donuts were going through their first proofing, a routine that had become habit over the years. "Do you ever get tired of washing dishes and cleaning up around here, Emma?" I asked her.

"Let me ask you something instead of answering you directly. Do you ever get tired of making donuts?" she asked with a smile.

"No, not really."

"Me, either. I perform a needed and useful task, and I'm part of the team that brings smiles all over April

Springs and beyond. How could anyone ever get tired of that? Besides, you let me listen to whatever music I prefer at the moment, and I have time to think deep thoughts when I'm buried up to my elbows in warm, sudsy water. In a lot of ways, this is the perfect job for me, Suzanne."

"I'm glad that you feel that way," I said as I started adding flour, salt, and yeast into my large stand mixer.

"I am, too," she said. "Do you think they'll still be out there when we take our break?"

"It's a murder crime scene; I have a hunch that they're going to be there awhile." I looked at the donuts resting on the drip trays as I added, "As a matter of fact, I made extras, so let's take a dozen across the street on our break. How does that sound to you?"

"I think it's really nice," she said. "Maybe we can even get a little inside scoop while we're there."

"Emma, let's leave the questions to your father. I'd really rather not get involved if I can help it."

When I looked at her, she just grinned at me. "What's so funny?"

"Suzanne, forgive me, but is there one chance in a hundred that you're not going to end up investigating Zane Dunbar's murder?"

I shook my head sadly. "We both know the answer to that, don't we?" I had other reasons besides curiosity to figure out why someone had killed Zane. I hadn't liked the way Grace's face had turned so pale the night before when he'd whispered something in her ear, and I had a hunch that my best friend might be considered a suspect the moment that Chief Martin found out about the exchange. I was sure he would soon start interviewing witnesses from the reunion, no doubt starting with Officer Stephen Grant himself.

The dough for the yeast donuts was ready to proof, so I covered the top and then I grabbed a tray of donuts. "I'm going to box these up, and then we can walk over there together."

"I'm way ahead of you," Emma said as she pulled out a folded box all ready to fill.

As we walked through the kitchen and out into the front, I tucked the donuts under my arm and reached for the door. One glance outside told me that Ray Blake was still over there talking to the police chief. I hoped that Chief Martin didn't blame me for it, but it couldn't be helped. I needed the head lawman's cooperation, but that didn't mean that I owed Emma anything less. Hopefully Ray wouldn't make a scene when we got over there, but I wouldn't put it past him. The man believed in his heart that he was a grizzled old newshound, even if his paper *did* feature more advertisements than stories. Honestly, what newspaper didn't these days? Still, he pressed folks around April Springs a lot harder than he probably should, and one day it was going to backfire on him.

I just hoped that day wasn't today.

Chapter 3

"Sorry, but I can't chat. I have a story to file," Ray said as he blew past Emma and me. I *knew* that he was in a hurry because he didn't even try to grab a free donut from the box I was carrying.

"Hang on a second, Dad," Emma said. "I want to talk to you."

"That's fine, but you'd better make it quick," he said.

"This is important," Emma answered, and the two of them stepped away from the crime scene and closer to Ray's car.

"Do I even have to *ask* you how that just went?" I asked Chief Martin as he approached.

"I'm pretty sure that you can use your imagination," he said.

"I brought donuts for you and your crew," I said as I held them out.

"You know how I feel about taking freebies from anyone," the chief said reluctantly as he studied my offerings.

"I get it, but this is different, Chief."

"How's that?" he asked.

"If you don't take them, I'll just have to throw them out," I said. I had a policy that once a donut went into a box, it never touched my shelves again. I knew that there was nothing wrong with these donuts, but it was a rule that I stuck to, no matter what.

"Well, we can't have that," he said as he reached for the box. "Thanks."

"You're welcome," I said. I gestured to where the body had been slumped over earlier. One of Chief Martin's officers was unbolting the entire bench from its concrete foundation. "Are you taking *everything*?"

"We have to; it's evidence. Don't worry. Parks and

Rec will be coming by in an hour to replace it. You don't want that reminder staring at you every time you walk out the door anyway, do you?"

"No, I think that it's a fine idea to remove it all at that," I said. "Have you learned anything new since I was over here earlier with the coffee?"

"You know how it goes, Suzanne. We collect all of the information that we can and then we analyze it later. Right now we're just trying to make sure that we don't miss anything."

I pointed to two officers making an ever-widening circle around the bench, studying the ground in front of them carefully.

"What are they hoping to find?"

"Well, I won't lie to you. A clue would be nice," he said. "I really wish that you had a security camera out front."

He'd made the same suggestion half a dozen times in the past, but I'd always had to say no. "I'm running a pretty fine line between red and black ink as it is. A security system would put me over that line farther than I'd be comfortable with."

"I get that," he said. "The good news is that we should be finished up before you open."

"That's great," I said, and I meant it. The last thing I needed was a full-scale murder investigation going on across the street from my donut shop. The chief was right. I didn't need any more reminders than I already had about what had happened to Zane. The memory of finding him was more than enough to give me nightmares.

"We do what we can," he said.

I was about to say something when the officer working on removing the bench called over to us. "Chief, if you've got a second, I could use a hand."

"Be right there," he said, and then he turned to me. "Duty calls. Thanks again for the donuts."

"It was the least I could do," I answered.

"No, the *least* you could have done was stand over there in the window and watch us work."

"I've always been more of a doer, myself," I said, regardless of what Zane had said to me the night before. "You know that."

"As a matter of fact, I do," he said with a slight smile.

After the police chief went over to help remove the bench, I started back to the shop. Emma caught up with me before I made it to the front door.

"What was that all about with your father?" I asked her.

"Dad's being stuffy about me going back to college again," she said. Ray hadn't been all that thrilled when Emma had come home, and he hadn't been shy about sharing that opinion with her on a nearly daily basis.

"What did you say?" I asked as I unlocked our front door.

"I told him that things could be worse. I'm taking classes at the community college, aren't I? If he keeps pushing me, I might just move away from April Springs and *never* go back to college."

"Emma, you wouldn't do that, would you?" I asked. I understood that someday Emma would leave Donut Hearts again and head back to school for good, but I hated the thought of her leaving me just to get away from her father's nagging.

"Of course I wouldn't. I was only bluffing," she said with a grin.

"So did it work?"

She shrugged. "Only time will tell, but don't worry. *Nobody's* getting rid of me that easily."

"I should hope not," I said as I put an arm around her. "Truth be told, I've kind of gotten used to having you around."

"Thanks. I'm happy here, too. So what should we do next?"

I pretended to consider it, and then I said, "It might be a

good idea to get cracking on those yeast donuts."

"You're such a slave driver," Emma said with a smile.

"You don't have to tell me that. Nobody knows it better than I do. At least you've got the option to just walk away if things get too bad here. Me, I'm in it for the long haul."

"Don't write me off just yet," she said as we put our aprons back on. "I've got a lot of donutmaking still ahead of me."

"I certainly hope so," I said as I approached the dough still resting in the floor mixer. It was time to get started again, and I was glad that I had the distraction of donutmaking to take my mind off what had happened to Zane Dunbar. I wondered how Janet was holding up, and I promised myself that I'd track her down and see if there was anything I could do to help her through her grief.

In the meantime, it was time to make the donuts yet again.

"You're *never* going to believe who's out front waiting to get in," Emma said hours later when we were ten minutes from opening Donut Hearts for the day. She'd been in front getting ready for our day while I'd stayed in back, working until the last possible second. Once upon a time, we'd been open at five AM every day, but I'd decided to change it to six in order to come in an hour later so I could get a little more sleep. A few of our regulars had complained about it, but they'd quickly gotten used to the new hours. I'd also started shutting down at eleven instead of noon, and so far, I hadn't had many complaints about that, either. It still made for a long day at the donut shop, but at least now it was more doable. It was amazing how much difference an hour here and there could mean, and I knew that unless I was in dire financial straits, I'd never go back to the old system.

"Is it our fair mayor?" I asked as I finished the last-minute prep work in the kitchen. George had been known to visit us early, but it was still unusual enough to comment on.

"No, it's Grace," Emma said.

I dropped the pan I'd been taking to the sink and brushed past her. "And you didn't let her in?"

"No, why would I? It wasn't time to open yet. *Should* I have?" Emma asked me.

"I'll take care of it," I said. Had Grace already heard what had happened to Zane? Why else would she be here?

"I'm really sorry. I didn't even think about it," Emma said.

"It's fine, but I'm going to go let her in. Would you mind finishing up those dishes?"

"I'm on it," she said. That would keep her in the kitchen until we were ready to open, giving her something to do and allowing Grace and me some privacy to talk.

As I opened the door, I saw Grace rubbing her hands together. "It's a little chilly out there this morning, isn't it?" she asked me. "Is it six already?"

"No, it's ten 'til," I said. "Get in here. I've got coffee."

"Are you sure?"

"Grace," I said as I motioned her inside, and she obeyed. I kept the CLOSED sign in the door, so if anyone else came early and saw us, I'd just point to it and then to the clock. It was capricious of me letting Grace in and no one else, but like Trish at the Boxcar, I was the ruler of my own dominion, and for once, I'd do what I wanted to and forget about what my customers might desire.

"Coffee?" I asked her as I poured two cups without waiting for a response from her.

"Yes, please," she said.

"I'm guessing you heard about Zane," I said.

After Grace took a long sip, she nodded. "I heard about

it on the radio this morning."

"You're usually not an early riser by choice," I said as casually as I could muster.

"To be honest with you, I had trouble sleeping last night," Grace admitted, and then she looked back toward the kitchen. "Suzanne, can we talk?"

"Relax. Emma's doing dishes right now, and unless I miss my guess, she's got her music cranked up too high to overhear us."

"Would you mind checking anyway?" Grace asked.

I nodded as I turned and opened the kitchen door. As I suspected, Emma was buried in the sink up to her arms, and her earbuds were firmly in place. I ducked back out again before she could see me and told Grace, "We're good. What do you want to talk about?"

"I need to tell you what Zane said to me last night that shook me up so much," Grace said.

"Don't feel like you have to, but if you're sure you want to, then I'd be happy to listen."

"Before I get into all of that, there's something else that you should know first."

"Go ahead," I said as I took another sip of my coffee. We didn't exactly have all morning, but I didn't feel right about pushing Grace, either. If I had to delay opening to hear what she had to say, then so be it.

"I went back to the reunion last night after you left," she admitted a little guiltily.

"Why would you do that?" I asked, forgetting myself for a second.

"I couldn't stand the thought of letting Zane think that he'd rattled me," she said.

"Even though it was clear that he did just that," I replied.

Grace shrugged. "Of course he did, but I didn't want him to feel as though he had any power over me anymore."

I wasn't exactly sure what she meant by that, but I

sensed that this wasn't the time to question her. "What happened?"

"When I got there, he was arguing with Mr. Davidson."

"Our old English teacher?" I asked.

"One and the same. He told Zane that he would regret something, but when he saw me, he left without another word."

"I wonder what that was about?"

"I didn't have a clue, nor did I care at the time, either. I just wanted to talk to Zane."

"Grace, you're going to have to tell me what happened so I'll be able understand all of this."

She took a deep breath, and then let it out slowly. "I know. The truth is, I'm *embarrassed* to tell you."

I stepped around the counter and took her hands in mine. "Grace, there's *nothing* that you can say to me that will make me think any less of you."

"Don't be so sure of that," Grace said. She looked as though she were about to burst into tears. Whatever it was, it was clearly deeply troubling to her.

"Go on. You can trust me," I said.

"Okay, here goes. When I was sixteen, I shoplifted a necklace from Dunbar's Jewelers. It was just under a hundred dollars, and back then I never thought I'd ever have that much to my name, and I really wanted it. It was a stupid impulse, something I immediately regretted. I didn't think anyone saw it, but evidently Zane did. I didn't even remember him being in the store that day. Anyway, I put it away in one of my drawers and I *never* wore it. The *only* reason that I kept it was because I was too embarrassed to give it back. Besides, it helped me remember to ignore stupid ideas, so in a way, it helped me grow up."

"Grace, you shouldn't keep beating yourself up over it. Everyone does things they're ashamed of at one time or another in their lives."

"Even you?" she asked me sincerely.

"More than I can list," I said.

"I think you're just trying to make me feel better, but there's nothing that you can do to make that happen. I always felt bad about it, and I considered paying the Dunbars for it a hundred times over before they died in that car crash. Then I knew that I'd just have to live with what I'd done. Honestly, I'd almost forgotten about it until Zane brought it up again last night. He threatened to tell everyone in town what I'd done, and I froze, Suzanne. Knowing that he could hurt my reputation was almost more than I could take. Ever since I took that necklace, I've made it a point to be honest to the point of pain, you know? It's not fair that he was about to ruin everything that I'd worked so hard for."

"So why did you go back last night?" I asked, not sure that I really wanted the answer anymore. I knew in my heart that Grace couldn't kill anyone, but if she felt as though she needed to defend her honor and her good name, she might be pushed into doing something that she'd later regret.

"I grabbed the necklace from the hiding place I'd been keeping it in and I went back to return it. I knew that it wouldn't make up for what I'd done, but I couldn't stand the thought of having it anymore. When I tried to give it back to Zane, he just laughed at me! He said that it would take more than the necklace's return to buy his silence, but what he was demanding from me, I wasn't willing to give."

"I can only guess what he wanted."

"You're going to have to, because I'm not about to repeat it. When I said no, Zane threw the necklace at me and called me a liar and a thief."

"What did you do?" I asked her.

"What could I do? I started to go, but then I heard shouting behind me. Evidently Mr. Davidson had found Zane again, and he still had his own bone to pick with the man. He kept shouting something about Helen Marston, and that he was going to defend her honor. I heard Zane say that he was much too late for that, and then Mr. Davidson attacked him! He tackled Zane right there in the parking lot, and it took three guys to pull him off. Zane was as mad as I'd ever seen him, and he started telling Mr. Davidson that he was a dead man. He was shouting it, actually."

"How did Mr. Davidson react to that?" I asked. It was hard to imagine our old English teacher in a brawl.

"He tried to break free of the guys restraining him, and as he struggled, he kept saying, 'This isn't over, not by a long shot. I'll bury you if I have to, Zane!'" Grace shivered a little as she retold it, and it felt as though I was there, myself. It must have been some kind of scene.

"So then you went back home?"

"I swear, I came straight back. I'll admit that I didn't get much sleep last night, but I felt as though I did what I had to do by giving that necklace back to him."

"Where is it now?" I asked her.

"I have no idea. For all I know, it's still lying there in the parking lot. Why?"

"Think about it, Grace. It's got your fingerprints on it, and Zane's as well. Don't you think Chief Martin might want to know what that's all about?"

Her face suddenly went white. "I hadn't even thought about that. Suzanne, what am I going to do?"

I thought about it for a few seconds, and then I said, "The chief's still at the crime scene across the street, but I don't know how much longer he's going to be there. You and I need to go over there right now and tell him everything that happened last night."

"*Everything*?" Grace asked. "Suzanne, if I tell him the truth, he's going to arrest me for stealing that necklace."

"Think about it, Grace. The statute of limitations *has* to have run out on that crime. If I remember correctly, they only have two years to arrest you after something like that. If it's true, then he *can't* arrest you for stealing that necklace."

"Even if you're right, it's not something I want to admit to the police chief."

"I understand that, but it's going to be a lot worse if they find that necklace and he comes to you asking about it." I put a hand on her shoulder. "Grace, the sooner you get this over with, the better. I'll come with you, and I'll be right by your side the entire time. What do you say?"

Grace considered it for a few seconds, and then she nodded. "If you'll go with me, I'll do it. But what about the donut shop?"

"Emma can handle the front," I said. "Give me one second, and don't go anywhere."

"I promise. Suzanne, thanks for standing by me."

"There was never any question of it," I said, and then did my best to offer a comforting smile. "It'll be okay, Grace. Trust me."

"I really hope you're right," she said.

I went into the kitchen and tapped Emma on the shoulder. She turned off her music and asked, "Is it time to open yet?"

"It is," I said. "And I need a favor."

"You know that all you have to do is ask," she said.

"Run the front when we open. I'm going to do something with Grace, but I shouldn't be too long."

"Okay, I can handle that," she said. I knew that it wasn't Emma's favorite task around Donut Hearts, but she was always ready to step in when I needed her, and that meant even at the spur of the moment like right now.

"Thanks. Good luck."

"You bet," she said as she walked out front with me.

"I'm so sorry I left you waiting outside earlier," Emma said to Grace as we walked out together.

"It was no problem, Emma. Honestly, I didn't mind waiting," she said.

"Still, it won't happen the next time."

"I hope there isn't ever going to *be* a next time," Grace

said.

"I totally get that," Emma said.

"Let's go," I said to Grace as I unlocked the door and switched the sign to OPEN. There were already a few folks waiting in line to get donuts, and I could see Emma take a deep breath.

"Are you going to be okay?" I asked her.

"I'll be fine," she said. "Go."

"We will," I said as Grace and I left Donut Hearts.

"What did you say to her?" Grace asked me as we made our way through the waiting customers.

"I just asked her to watch the front," I explained.

"You didn't say why, did you?"

"Grace, she works for me. I don't have to justify every request I make of her. Emma doesn't mind watching the front while we do this."

"Thanks for keeping my secret," Grace said.

"I was happy to do it, but you know that the chief isn't going to make any promises, don't you?" I hated saying it, but I didn't want my friend blindsided when word got out, as no doubt it soon could.

"I know, and I'm willing to accept the consequences," Grace said.

"Relax," I said as I squeezed her shoulder. "Nobody's going to jail, at least not for this."

"That helps a little, I guess," she said, but as we approached the chief, who was standing near his squad car, I could feel her tense up beside me.

"Grace, just tell him the story the exact same way that you told me and you'll be fine."

"Okay," I said.

"Chief, do you have a second?" I asked as we reached him.

"Sure, but not much more than that. Just because we're finished up here doesn't mean that there's not a great deal of work still ahead of us. This investigation isn't going to be easy; I can feel it in my bones."

"This involves what happened last night," I said. "At least indirectly."

"Let's hear it, then."

I turned to Grace and nodded, and she began to speak. After she was finished, I squeezed her hand, and then I turned back to the chief. "Have you found the necklace yet?"

"As a matter of fact, we did," he said. "Grace, don't be so hard on yourself. Kids can do stupid things sometimes. I'm not condoning shoplifting, but I know that's not who you are."

"I'm so sorry," she said, nearly in tears from the emotion of retelling her story. "If I could do it all over again, I would never go a hundred feet within that store, and that's the truth."

"I believe you," he said.

"Chief, does *everyone* have to know about this?" I asked.

He frowned for a moment, and then he shrugged. "At this point, I don't see why they should. I won't add it to my reports right away unless it becomes relevant later."

"Do you think I could have killed Zane?" Grace asked him in bewilderment.

"I'm not going to comment on that until I've gathered quite a bit more information than I have right now."

"She's been fully cooperative, though, and she even gave you more names of people to look at," I said. "Surely that ought to count for something."

"Of course it does," Chief Martin said. "I just told you that I'll keep this between us for now. What more can you ask than that?"

"You could say that you don't think Grace killed Zane Dunbar," I said.

Before he could answer, it was Grace's turn to squeeze my hand. "Suzanne, we both know that he can't say that, at least not yet. He's promised to keep my secret for now. That's more than I was hoping for."

"Thanks for understanding," the chief said.

"You don't have any other choice," Grace said.

"It's probably crazy of me to even ask this, but you two are going to investigate this murder yourselves, aren't you?" Chief Martin asked.

"Do we have any real choice?" I asked.

"I know that *you* don't think that you do," he said. "You both need to be careful, though, and keep me informed about what you find. Is that a deal?"

"It is," I said, and Grace agreed.

"Then go on and let me get back to work," the chief said with the hint of a smile. He paused before he got into his car and looked at Grace. "Don't worry. If that's the worst of it, you're going to be fine."

"Thanks again," she said.

After he was gone, Grace added, "You want to know something? He's not so bad after all, is he?"

"I told you that he's mellowed quite a bit lately."

"That's not going to keep us from digging into Zane's death ourselves though, is it?" she asked me.

"Grace, you heard what I told him. We don't really have any choice. As a matter of fact, if you're game, I might have Emma run the shop by herself today so we can start interviewing some of our suspects right away."

"Are you sure she won't mind?" Grace asked.

"As long as I don't make a habit of it, she'll be fine," I said.

"That would be great," she said.

"Wait right here then. I'll be right back."

I walked back into the donut shop, and Emma said, "That was quick. Are you two finished already?"

"I'm sorry to tell you this, but we're going to need more time. Do you mind holding down the fort a little longer?"

"How long are we talking about?" she asked me.

"The rest of the day, actually."

Emma frowned, and then she asked, "Could I call my

mom to come in and help?"

"She wouldn't mind?" I asked.

"Are you kidding? She'd love it."

"Then go ahead and give her a call," I said. "Thanks for doing this, Emma."

"Happy to help. Good luck," she said as I started for the door.

"With what?" I asked her. I hadn't told her that Grace and I would be investigating the murder, but then again, it probably wasn't that big a leap for her to figure it out on her own.

"You know," she answered with a grin.

"I do, and thanks," I said.

Grace was waiting patiently for me outside. "Are you ready?" she asked me.

"Well, it's just past six AM, so I'm not sure how many of our suspects are even awake yet, but I'm ready if you are."

"Maybe we'll be able to catch them off guard this early in the day," she said.

"If we're lucky," I answered. "The reunion booked rooms at the Bentley Hotel in Union Square, so that's probably the best place to start."

"Let's go, then," she said, and we got into my Jeep and headed for the town next to ours. "Suzanne, as of right now, I'm on vacation until further notice."

"You don't even have to ask anyone?" I asked her.

"I've got some latitude taking time off," she said.

"That must be nice."

"Why do you say that? You can take off whenever you want," Grace said.

"Maybe in theory, but we both know how many times I've taken advantage of that."

"Not nearly enough," Grace agreed.

Chapter 4

It was a little after seven when we got to the Bentley Hotel. It was nice, never part of a chain, and it had an older elegance about it that I liked. I'd never stayed there since I lived just one town away, but I'd eaten there with Momma a few times over the years, always on special occasions. As a matter of fact, I'd taken her there this past Mother's Day, and we'd had quite a nice time enjoying their Sunday-afternoon fete.

"Suzanne, it's so early, do you think anyone will even be awake, given that the reunion just happened last night? And even if they are, how are we going to know if they're up yet?"

"That part's easy enough," I said as I headed left toward the restaurant entrance instead of right to the front desk. "We'll see who's eating breakfast and go from there."

"I never even thought of that," Grace said. "That's probably why *you're* the lead detective."

"Funny, but I like to think that we're *co-conspirators*," I said.

"Ooh, I like *your* word for us better," she said. As we approached the maître d's stand, Grace asked me, "Is that Janet and Billy Briscoe eating? What are they doing sitting together?"

"Didn't you know?" I asked. "They were hot and heavy at the end of school right before we all graduated. I wonder why they split up?"

"Maybe she got some taste?" Grace asked.

"Then how do you explain how she ended up with Zane?" I asked softly.

"So much for not speaking ill of the dead," Grace said.

"I've never been much of a believer in that custom," I said. "We both know what kind of man he was, and the fact that he's dead now doesn't really change that one bit, does it?"

"Maybe not, but I'd probably pick a different way to approach the subject with his widow."

"You know that I will," I said.

"Just checking," Grace said. "Are you ready to talk to them?"

"Ready as I'll ever be," I said as Grace and I walked over there together. No one had come to the hostess's station while we'd been standing there, so it must be self-seating this early in the morning.

"May we join you?" I asked as Grace and I got to their table.

They clearly hadn't seen us coming. Billy looked startled to suddenly find us standing there, and Janet looked absolutely mortified.

"We're not together," Janet said quickly as she pushed her plate away from Billy's. Her eyes were red and puffy from crying, and she looked as though she hadn't slept all night. "He just came over to offer me his condolences, but he has to go now." With that, she turned to him and added, "You *do* have to go, *don't* you? Thanks again for stopping by."

"Happy to do it," Billy said as he stood. He looked awkwardly around for a second, and then he said, "If you all will excuse me, I have a few telephone calls to make."

I wasn't about to let him go that easily. "Billy, what's your room number? After Grace and I speak with Janet, we'd like to have a chat with you."

"I can't imagine why you'd want to do that," he said.

"Trust me, you'll *want* to talk to us," Grace said in a way that made it sound as though it would be in his best interest to cooperate. I didn't know how she did it, but my best friend was really good with tone and inflection, and she had a way of sounding as though she always knew exactly what she was doing. It was something that I admired greatly.

Reluctantly, he admitted, "I'm in 207," and then he left us.

"May we sit with you a moment?" I asked Janet.

"I'm really not in the mood for company," she said as she managed to look uncomfortable by our very presence.

"We understand completely, but don't worry. We won't stay long," Grace said as she took Billy's old seat. I wasn't one to ordinarily press people so hard, but this was important, so I took the closest seat on Janet's other side.

"First of all, we're both so sorry for your loss," I said.

"Yes, we were deeply troubled by it," Grace added, making Janet whipsaw her head from one of us to the other.

After a moment, she gave up on doing that altogether and focused directly on me. "I understand that you're the one who found…him."

"I did," I said.

"It must have been terrible for you," Janet said with real sympathy in her voice.

"It was pretty bad," I agreed. "When did you see your husband last?" I asked.

"When we danced at the reunion, of all things," she said. "Zane wasn't a very big fan of dancing, but I'd made him promise to share at least one dance with me, and he made good on his word. At least I got the chance to be held in his arms one last time." She looked as though she wanted to cry again, and given what she'd been through recently, I couldn't really blame her.

"Do you happen to remember exactly what time your last dance was?" Grace asked.

Janet glanced over at Grace briefly before she said, "You'd have to ask the DJ. It was the last song they played last night."

"So then, you two didn't leave together?" I asked her.

"Zane sent me back here to the hotel," she said. "He told me that he'd catch a ride with someone else, that he had some unfinished business to take care of, and that I shouldn't worry about how late he came in. He said it all so matter-of-factly that I didn't even question it. Zane was like that, strong and forceful when he needed to be."

"Do you have any idea who he might have been talking about?" I asked her.

"There were several folks at the reunion last night who had issues with my husband. I wouldn't even know where to begin."

"How about with Billy Briscoe?" Grace asked, and that got her another full stare.

"I'm sure I don't know what you're talking about."

"Well, I saw Billy and Zane arguing last night. It's kind of odd to find him sitting at your table this morning, don't you think?"

"Billy was drunk, and he picked a fight with Zane, along with half a dozen other people at the reunion. He apologized to me, and I told him that all was forgiven. They weren't the best of friends before Zane and I got together, and it didn't help matters when we got married."

"Was Billy still in love with you after all these years?" I asked her.

Janet blushed slightly, and then she tried to hide it with her napkin. "That was a long time ago."

"Maybe the reunion brought old feelings back to the surface again," Grace said. "It must have been hard for him to see you and Zane together."

"That's nonsense," Janet said.

"Maybe, maybe not, but *someone* killed your husband," I said, "and we aim to find out who did it."

Janet was shocked by the suggestion that Grace and I would investigate a murder. "You two? Suzanne, you run a donut shop, and Grace, the last I heard you worked for a cosmetics company. What makes either one of you think that you're qualified to solve a murder?"

"Past experience," I said. "You should know that

Grace and I have cracked more than our share of homicide cases over the years."

"Well, I don't want you digging into Zane's death, do you understand me?" she asked huffily.

Grace asked, "Gosh, Janet, we thought that you'd *want* to see your husband's killer found."

"Of course I do, but by the police, not by a couple of amateurs."

"Be that as it may, we're going to investigate anyway," I said firmly.

"We'll see about that. I'll have a word with the police chief."

"Have as many as you want," Grace said. "But I should warn you, it's not going to help."

She didn't know quite what to make of that, so Janet stood and threw her napkin down on the table. "If you'll excuse me, I have funeral arrangements to make."

"Are you leaving the county soon, Janet?" I asked her as we stood as well.

"No, Zane always wanted to be buried here beside his parents. I'll be in the area for the next few days arranging things, and then I'm never coming back to April Springs."

"I'm sure that we'll have the opportunity to speak again in the meantime," Grace said.

Janet didn't even answer; she just left us in a snit. Was her anger just an excuse to get away from us, or was it a way to deal with what had happened to her husband? I knew from experience that folks acted differently when they lost someone they loved, and some of them lashed out at the nearest punching bag. Then again, she'd been pretty adamant about Grace and me butting out. Maybe she had something to hide herself, or perhaps she didn't want us uncovering someone close to her as the killer. None of it was going to change anything, though. Grace and I would keep digging until we found the truth, and a few complaints to the police chief weren't about to change that.

The waitress came by with the bill and looked puzzled when she saw that Janet and Billy were gone. "I cannot believe that they left without paying," she said.

"Charge it to Room 207. Billy Briscoe," Grace said confidently.

The waitress frowned for a moment. "Actually, we're supposed to get a signature on the check as well in case there is a dispute later."

"I'll take care of that," Grace said as she took the slip of paper and scrawled out a name before handing it back to the server. "How's that?"

The waitress stared at it for a few seconds, and then she said, "I have no idea what that says."

"Then neither will your boss," Grace said with a smile.

"Okay, I suppose that's good enough for me. May I get you two anything?"

It was tempting, but Grace and I had work to do. Our growling stomachs would just have to wait. "Thanks, but we're good."

As she left, Grace asked, "Suzanne, why did you do that? We could have had a free breakfast on Billy Briscoe."

"Don't you think that he might have noticed? I doubt that he'll balk at paying for Janet, but four breakfasts on his bill might be a little too much for him to take, don't you think?"

"I suppose," Grace said. "Are we off to tackle Billy now?"

"We are, unless there's someone else you'd like to speak with first."

"No, I think Billy Briscoe belongs high on our list, given what we just saw this morning."

"You know," I said as we made our way out of the restaurant to the hotel proper, "it might all turn out to be perfectly innocent."

"It might be, but what good does it do us to assume

that?" she asked.

"No good at all. How should we approach Billy?"

"Well, we could start with the way he spoke with you last night at the reunion," Grace answered.

"Come on, he wasn't *that* bad," I said.

"Maybe not, but what are the chances that he'll remember that?"

"Not very good," I said with a smile. "Okay, I'm willing to play along to see what else we might find out."

"Then let's go," Grace said.

We didn't make it to Billy's room though, at least not without interruption. At the front desk, we ran into someone else who had to be on our list, even if Grace might not be too keen about it.

And from the bag at his feet and the bill in his hand, it appeared that Tom Hancock was leaving town.

"Going somewhere?" I asked Tom as we detoured over to the desk.

"The reunion's over," he told me, and then he turned to Grace. "I'm sorry about the way things ended last night."

"So am I," Grace said. "Do you really have to go right now?"

"There's nothing keeping me here, is there?" he asked, looking hopefully into her eyes.

She was about to answer when I heard a familiar voice. "Mr. Hancock, excuse me, but I need a word with you."

It was Chief Martin, and while he didn't look all that surprised seeing Grace and me standing there, he didn't look particularly pleased by it, either.

"Sheriff, what can I do for you?" Tom asked.

"It's Chief," he corrected him. "I was kind of hoping that you'd stick around a little longer, given the circumstances."

"What circumstances are those?" Tom asked as he signed his bill with a flourish.

"Murder," Chief Martin said.

That caught Tom off-guard. "Murder? Who was murdered?"

"Are you saying that you haven't heard?" Grace asked him.

"I haven't heard a thing. I got up, showered, and then I packed my bag. I didn't speak with anyone on the way down here, and no one's mentioned murder to me. I repeat, who was murdered?"

I was about to tell him when the chief spoke up first. "Somebody killed Zane Dunbar in front of the donut shop last night, and I've heard from three separate witnesses that you had a fight with the man last night soon before he died."

"It wasn't a fight, not really," Tom said, speaking quickly. "He took a swing at me while I was dancing, I avoided it, and he fell on the floor. It was all just an innocent misunderstanding." Tom turned to Grace as he added, "You can ask her. She was standing right next to me when it happened."

"How about it, Grace? Was it really all that innocent?"

Grace couldn't even meet Tom's gaze as she answered, "What he didn't mention was that they had a few heated words. It wasn't innocent at all, if you want my honest opinion."

Tom looked surprised by her statement. "Come on, Grace, that's not the way it was, and you know it. What about what Zane said to you? You looked as though you'd been slapped in the face when he whispered something in your ear."

"I already know all about that," Chief Martin said quickly. "We're talking about you right now."

"I didn't kill the man," Tom said fiercely.

"When's the last time you saw him?" the chief asked.

"On the dance floor, when I was with Grace," he said.

"Can anyone else confirm that?"

"It's nearly impossible to prove the negative," Tom

replied. "Of course I can't prove that we didn't speak again. All I can give you is my word."

"I can see your point," Chief Martin said, "but if it's all the same to you, I'd appreciate it if you'd stick around for the next two or three days until we get this cleared up."

"What makes you think you can solve his murder so quickly?" Tom asked, pointedly ignoring both of us now.

"Why don't we revisit that in three days and see where we stand then?"

"Is that an order?"

"Think of it more as a strongly worded request," the chief said.

"Fine," Tom said as he turned back to the clerk, who'd been discreetly listening to every word of our conversation. "It appears that I'll need my room for two more nights after all."

"Yes, sir," she said as she started the process of his extension.

"If that's all," Tom said when he got his room key back, "I'll be off."

"We appreciate your cooperation," the chief said automatically.

"Of course," Tom answered as he brushed past us both.

"Sorry about that," the chief said after Tom Hancock was gone. "I didn't mean to put you on the spot like that."

"It wasn't your fault," Grace said. "You asked me a fair question, and I told you the truth."

"It didn't make you very popular with Tom Hancock though, did it?"

"Don't worry about it, Chief."

"If you say so," he said. "Who *else* have you two spoken with since I left you?"

I smiled. "Don't act shocked and surprised. You *knew* that we were going to investigate."

"I did, but I figured I had at least until the donut shop closed for the day. You didn't shut it down completely, did you?"

"No, Emma and her mother are running it today."

The chief whistled. "Suzanne, you're not playing around here, are you? I've never known you to drop Donut Hearts for a murder investigation."

"What can I say? It's important to us. We've already started a suspect list."

"Go ahead, then. Give me some names."

I told him about our earlier conversation with the widow, and our plans to speak with Billy Briscoe next. "I'm guessing that you don't want us talking to Billy before you do, though, is that right?" I asked.

"On the contrary, I think that you should both go speak to him right now," the chief said.

"Are you sure?" I asked.

"Why do you ask?"

"It's just not like you to give us a green light to speak to someone that you haven't questioned yet," I said.

"Maybe I want you to break the ice with him first, and then I'll follow up before he has a chance to collect his wits."

"Are we playing 'good cop bad, cop' here?" Grace asked with a smile.

"No, mostly because you two aren't cops," the chief said. "I just think this one time in particular that it might not be a bad idea for you to go first, unless you don't want to."

"We want to," I said as I tugged at Grace's arm. "Come on, let's go."

"Call me the second that you're finished with him," the chief said.

"We will," I said as Grace and I headed down the hallway to room 207.

"Why did he have a sudden change of heart like that?" Grace asked me as we hurried toward Billy's door.

"I'm not sure, and I don't want to give him any time to second-guess his decision," I said.

We were there, so Grace said, "Then it might not be a bad idea to go ahead and knock."

"Here goes nothing," I said, and I tapped lightly on Billy's door.

Chapter 5

Of course he didn't answer.

"Knock again," Grace said.

I repeated it, but there still wasn't a response.

"Is he ignoring us, or is it something more sinister than that?" I asked Grace after another few moments.

"What do you mean? You don't think somebody might have killed him too, do you?"

"Not until you just said it I didn't," I said. "I was thinking more along the lines that he might have skipped town."

"Wouldn't he realize how that would make him look?" Grace asked me.

"Maybe he doesn't care," I said. "Let's go find the chief and see what he thinks."

Grace laughed a little as we made our way back to the reception area.

"What's so funny?" I asked her.

"Doesn't it strike *you* as a little odd that we're cooperating so fully with the police these days? When we first started investigating murder, we had to hide what we did from Chief Martin, and now it feels as though we're working hand in hand with him."

"I wouldn't go that far," I said as we came out into the lobby.

"Even you have to admit that it's not like it used to be," she said. "Hey, where did the chief go?" Grace asked as she looked around. He clearly wasn't in the lobby anymore.

"Maybe he got a bite to eat," I suggested, but a quick examination of the dining room gave the same results. The police chief was gone, just like Billy.

It was getting to be an epidemic.

"What should we do now?" Grace asked.

"I'm going to give him a call," I said as I pulled out my

phone.

"Billy?"

"No, not him. I don't have *his* number," I said as I hit the speed-dial for the police chief. "I'm calling Chief Martin."

"Okay, that makes sense."

"Martin," he said when he picked up.

"We can't find Billy Briscoe, and we can't find you, either."

"We're both out in the parking lot," the chief said. "He was going to slip away, but I convinced him to hang around a little bit longer." There was a hint of smugness in the police chief's voice, something that was easy to understand. He had power and authority that Grace and I could never have, using the force of the law to get what he wanted, while we had to finesse our way around most situations. It was just one more difference between us, a gap that would never be bridged. We might be cooperating more now than we ever had before, but there would never be a time where we were equals in anyone's eyes. Grace and I were good at what we did, getting people to open up to us about things they would never tell the police, but when it came right down to it, we didn't have any authority to make anyone do *anything* they didn't want to do.

"Should we come out there and join you?" I asked.

"There's really no need. Billy and I are going to go have a little chat somewhere more private."

"Are you taking him in?" I asked. I couldn't imagine how he could do that, not without a lot more evidence than he had at the moment.

"No, it's nothing like that. We're just going to grab a cup of coffee and have a little chat. I'll talk to you both later," he said, and then the police chief hung up on me.

"What did he say?" Grace asked as I put my phone away.

"He's got Billy, and they're going to go talk in private.

Oh, and we're not invited, either."

Grace frowned at that. "At least he didn't get away."

"We don't even know if he's *done* anything," I said. "Should we troll for more witnesses from last night while we're already here, or should we head back to April Springs and try to find Helen Marston and Mr. Davidson? What's his first name, anyway? It seems silly to keep calling an old teacher by his last name alone."

"Do you mean it's not Mister?" Grace asked with a smile.

"I doubt it," I said. "Remind me to ask him when we see him."

Grace nodded. "We might as well go do that now. There might be more people staying here who wanted to see something bad happen to Zane, but if there are, I don't know who they might be."

"It's settled, then. We head back to April Springs and ask our old teacher if he's a murderer."

"You've got to admit that we've had tougher conversations than that in the past," Grace offered.

"We have," I said, "but that doesn't mean that I'm looking forward to this one."

"Come on, it will be fine. Remember, I'll be right beside you all of the way."

"That's what I'm counting on," I said as we headed out to the parking lot to retrieve my Jeep. The chief was already gone, at least his squad car was, so I had to assume that he and Billy were about to have their own little chat. I would love to know what they were going to discuss, but unless the chief decided to share with me later, I doubted that Billy would tell me.

For the moment, I had my own set of problems.

"Helen, what are *you* doing here?" I asked Helen Marston after she answered Mr. Davidson's door. It was probably a stupid question to ask her, given that she was dressed only in a man's dress shirt, and she looked as though she'd just woken up.

"Suzanne, the real question is what are *you and Grace* doing here? Do you have any idea what time it is?"

"Trust me, we know. We've been up for hours already," Grace said. "Is Mr. Davidson around, or are you just housesitting for him?"

"Henry is in the shower," she said matter-of-factly.

"How long have you two been an item?" Grace asked her.

"We've been dating for several months," Helen said. "Grace, there's nothing wrong with me seeing an older man. After all, he hasn't been our teacher in quite a few years."

"Hey, date whoever you want," Grace said. "I'm happy when *anyone* finds love these days. Have you heard about Zane Dunbar?"

She nodded and managed to look sad. "We read about it in the paper this morning. It's tragic, isn't it?"

"It is," I said. "When did you see him last?"

Helen looked surprised by the question. "I don't know. I suppose it was at the reunion when everyone else did." She paused, and then looked back at Grace. "I heard that you had argued with him last night."

"We didn't argue," Grace said.

"That's not the way I heard it, but whatever," Helen said.

At that moment, Henry Davidson appeared, wearing the same suit and tie that he'd worn back when we'd been in school. "Ladies, what are you doing here?"

"We wanted to speak with you both about Zane Dunbar," I said.

"I don't know why," he replied, and then he turned to Helen and added, "Shouldn't you be getting dressed?"

"I've got loads of time yet," she said, clearly not taking the hint.

"Still, it might be prudent to go get ready now," Mr. Davidson said, and Helen nodded.

"Sure. Of course."

It was easy to picture them back when we'd all been in his class, but that was an image I now wanted to wipe from my mind. Helen was right. It had been too many years since he'd taught us to matter now, no matter how uncomfortable the thought of one of my old classmates dating our teacher might make me. Clearly it was my problem, not theirs.

Once Helen disappeared back inside, Mr. Davidson said, "I know that you girls have a reputation for investigating crime, but I assure you, I had nothing to do with Zane Dunbar's unfortunate demise." He said it in that lecturing voice I remembered all too well, one that didn't harbor any doubt or contradiction.

Well, we were a long way from being in his classroom at the moment, so the sooner he realized that, the better off we'd all be, as far as I was concerned. "Henry, you should know that it's not going to be as easy as all that. We're involved, and we expect answers from you, not lectures."

Mr. Davidson looked shocked by my rebellion, though Grace looked rather pleased with me.

It took the teacher a few moments to collect his composure, but when he did, it was clear that he was going to act as though he were still in charge, no matter how deluded he might be. "If you're going to take that attitude with me, then I'm afraid that I won't speak of this with you."

"Then you'll have to talk to Chief Martin," I said. "We were just trying to save you and Helen a little grief, that's all."

"What is that, a threat?" he asked, clearly unhappy that I was being so petulant. "Do you think that we're concerned that you might tell everyone about us?" He was defiant now, and I could see a streak of anger coming out in him that I'd never seen before. I'd been having a tough time seeing Mr. Davidson as someone capable of jamming a spear through someone's chest, but this man standing in front of me could have done it. Of that, there was no doubt in my mind.

"You should know that we don't threaten," I said, keeping my voice calm and level. "But then again, we don't bluff, either." At least not very often. I thought the last part instead of speaking it aloud, deciding to keep that little fact to myself.

"Tell the police chief, then. Tell the world for all that we care. We have nothing to hide, and nothing to be ashamed of. Just go away."

"Now is that any way for a teacher to act toward a couple of his favorite former students?" Grace asked him with a smile.

The slammed door in our face was answer enough.

We'd rattled Henry Davidson, there was no doubt about that, but was it because we'd caught him with Helen, or was it because he was guilty of something much worse than dating a former student?

Only time would tell.

"What should we do now?" I asked Grace. It was barely ten in the morning, and for as long as I could remember, I had been at the donut shop at that hour of the day. It felt positively bizarre not to be there right now. "Is there anyone else on our immediate list?"

Grace said, "No one that comes directly to mind." She looked a little uncomfortable as she said it, and I had to wonder if she was holding something back from me.

"Grace, what *aren't* you telling me? If it's about Zane's murder, or if it has anything to do with you, you need to come clean with me, and I mean one hundred percent."

"It's not about the case," she said softly.

"Whatever it involves, I want to know," I pressed a little harder.

"I feel guilty," she said.

I interrupted her before she could say anything else. "You might have had words with Zane last night, but we both know that you didn't kill him."

"It's not about that," she repeated. "I feel guilty about *you*."

That caught me off-guard. "Why would you feel guilty about *me*?"

"I need to go home and wrap a few things up before I can throw myself into this investigation," she said. "I've got an hour's worth of paperwork I need to file for my vacation time, and I also need to finish a few quarterly reports before I can take off."

"Why should that make you feel guilty toward me?" I asked, honestly puzzled by her statement.

"I asked you to leave the donut shop to investigate Zane's murder, and you walked away from it without a second thought, and here I am needing some time off to do my own job."

"In the first place, you didn't ask me; I volunteered, remember? And in the second place, I left my business in two sets of very capable hands, so it's not like I'm neglecting *anything*." I glanced at the clock on the dash, and then I added, "Why don't you go home, finish your work, and I'll swing by Donut Hearts to see if I can lend them a hand? We can meet back up at your place and go to lunch around eleven thirty. How does that sound to you?"

"Are you sure you aren't just trying to make me feel better?" Grace asked.

"Actually, I wouldn't mind a little physical confirmation that my donut shop hasn't burned down to the ground," I said.

"Do you honestly think that might happen?" she asked, looking surprised by the statement.

"No, but then again, I've never bailed out on it like this before. Who knows *how* the place will react?"

If Grace wondered about me referring to my business as

an actual person, she didn't comment on it. "If you're sure you don't mind, that sounds great."

"Let me drop you off at home," I said as I put the Jeep in gear.

"My car's at Donut Hearts, remember?" Grace asked.

"That's right; you were an early riser this morning, weren't you?"

"Don't remind me," she said as she stifled a yawn. "I just hope that I can stay awake long enough to do the paperwork on my desk at home."

"Take a twenty-minute power nap if you need to before you get to work. It does wonders for me some days."

"No, if I try to nap, I'll end up sleeping for days."

I knew that she wasn't being literal, but I wasn't about to comment. After we pulled into the parking area of Donut Hearts, I shut off the engine when I parked beside Grace's luxury company car.

"Here you go," I said as we both got out. "I'll see you soon."

"If I don't answer at the first knock, try a little harder the next time," she said with a grin as she got out her car keys. I knew that she was only partially kidding.

"Don't worry. You'll think you're in the middle of a thunderstorm if you don't answer the first time," I said with a grin.

After Grace pulled out of the parking area and headed home, I decided to peek into the donut shop instead of just barging in. After all, I'd asked Emma and her mother to step in for me at the last second, so a little chaos was to be expected.

When I looked through the window, fully expecting to see bedlam, I was a little disappointed to realize that they'd carried on admirably without me. The floor was swept, the tables cleaned, the counter gleamed, and the racks of donuts left in the displays were already consolidated. It was a little neater than I usually kept it myself, a fact that gave me some considerable reason to pause. I hated to admit it, even to myself, but it was hard for my ego to wrap itself around the truth: that I didn't have to be there every waking second for things to be all right.

I decided popping into Donut Hearts was the worst thing that I could do at the moment. It could easily be misread as me having a lack of faith in those two women, which was the last thing I wanted to convey. Turning around before anyone could spot me, I headed back toward my Jeep.

I didn't make it though, at least not before bumping into someone I hadn't expected to see anywhere near my donut shop.

Chapter 6

"Candy, what are you doing here?" I asked the woman I'd gone to high school with. "Did you come by my donut shop for a treat?" Candy Murphy been a freshman during my senior year, so we weren't all that close, but I'd known her from afar. Candy had been fond of wearing the most scandalous outfits she could get away with back then, and her taste in clothes hadn't changed much over the years. At the moment, she was wearing a mini-skirt I never would have dared to try on in my bedroom with the blinds pulled, and her top looked as though it had been meant for the high school freshman she'd been quite awhile ago. I had to admit that she still had the figure to pull it off, and I couldn't be completely certain that one of the reasons she could was because she hadn't stepped inside my donut shop a single time since I'd bought the place.

"I don't eat donuts, Suzanne," she said as though it were the most obvious thing in the world, which it probably was, when I thought about it. "You must know that I recently opened my own gym and spa. I just wish that I were as comfortable with my body as you seem to be with yours."

Was that a slam, or was she being serious? I looked into her eyes to see if she'd just zinged me, but I still couldn't tell. "You haven't gained a pound since high school," I said, merely stating another obvious fact.

"Actually, I've gained almost three," she said, clearly sad about this unfortunate development.

I decided not to share with her, or anyone else for that matter, exactly how many pounds I'd packed on over the years. Jake kept telling me that I shouldn't lose an ounce, and that he loved me exactly the way that I was, but I wasn't so sure, especially when I was around women like

Candy. "Well, I certainly can't tell by looking at you," I said.

She smiled broadly at my compliment. "Aren't you sweet."

"That's what happens when you run a donut shop. Candy, if you're not here for my donuts, then what can I do for you?"

She frowned before she said, "Let me ask you something first. Are you investigating Zane Dunbar's murder last night?"

"What makes you ask that?"

"Suzanne, everyone in town knows that you and Grace like to dig into murder cases on your own. What I need to know is if you've decided to investigate this one."

Apparently Candy was a little savvier than I'd given her credit for. "We might poke around the edges of the case," I reluctantly admitted.

"Good," she said. "I knew I came to the right place."

"Do you happen to know something about last night?" I asked her. I'd seen her at the multi-class reunion, dressed in her old prom dress of all things, but I had to admit that she'd looked spectacular in it.

"I do. I happened to see Zane arguing with Mr. Davidson about Helen Marston," she said as though she were delivering something truly significant.

"Yes, I heard," I said. "Grace and I spoke with them this morning. Did you know they were seeing each other?"

"I'd heard rumors," she replied, clearly a little disappointed that I'd learned something before she had. "How about Tom Hancock?" she asked. "He and Zane weren't on good terms at all." There was a spark of intelligence in her eyes as she said it, and I had to wonder if Candy had purposefully disguised a brain behind all that fluff she seemed to exude.

I hated to do it, but I had to burst her bubble again. "We knew that, too. Grace was dancing with Tom when he and Zane had their little tiff," I said.

"That's all I've got then," she said as she nodded. "Sorry, but I suppose I've bothered you for nothing."

"I appreciate the effort," I said.

Candy started to walk away, and then she stopped and turned back to me. "You haven't heard any rumors about me, have you, Suzanne?" The question was meant to be delivered casually, but she didn't quite pull it off.

"You? No. Why do you ask?"

"No reason. Well, I'm late for work," Candy said as she started to walk away. If she wore that outfit to her gym, I couldn't imagine what her workout clothes must be like.

As Candy pivoted the second time, she ran straight into our mayor's arms.

"I'm so sorry. I didn't see you there," Candy said as she stood there in very close proximity to my friend, George.

The mayor stammered as he tried to take a step back. "It was all my fault. I was on my cellphone and I didn't see you standing there. Forgive me."

Candy giggled a little, letting the intelligence I'd seen earlier slip back below the surface.

George took yet another step backward, and Candy finally released him. "I'll see you later, Mr. Mayor."

"Undoubtedly," George said, and we both watched Candy as she walked away with a little more swing in her step than was actually called for.

"What was that about?" I asked George with a grin as he turned back to me.

"What are you talking about?"

"I saw the way you blushed just then, so don't try to deny it," I said.

"She's quite lovely, and I still have a pulse, so yes, I noticed her. It's just a shame that she's not as smart as she is pretty."

I wasn't so sure about that, but I kept the observation to

myself. "What brings you here, your honor?"

"Suzanne, I heard that it was happening, but I had to see it for myself to believe it," George said.

"What are you talking about?" I asked him, Candy now forgotten.

"Someone told me that Emma and her mother were running Donut Hearts this morning. I laughed it off as a bad joke, but when someone else said the same thing, I had to find out if it was true for myself." He looked hard at me before he spoke again. "You're not ill, are you?"

"I've never felt better in my life, but thanks for asking," I said.

"So tell me this, Suzanne. If you're healthy and the donut shop is open for business, why aren't you inside waiting on customers?"

"Grace and I are investigating Zane Dunbar's murder," I said. I might not openly admit that to some folks in town, but not George. Before he'd become mayor, he'd helped Grace and me out quite a bit, and lately he'd even lent us a hand when we'd needed it, in spite of his title.

"I thought that must be it," the mayor said. "What can I do to help?"

"Nothing just yet, but we might need you again soon."

"I hope so," he said. "Sometimes I get bored just being the mayor around here."

"Enough that you want to rejoin our investigative team full time?" I asked him with a grin.

"With Polly holing up in Raleigh, I'll take any distractions that I can get." Polly North was his secretary/assistant in the mayor's office, and George's girlfriend, no matter how much he hated the term for a woman Polly's age. She'd gone to Raleigh to be with her new grandchild, but we'd all expected her back long before now.

"Isn't she ever coming back home?" I asked her.

"I asked the woman that exact question last night on the phone," George said.

"What did she say?"

"She was remarkably evasive, truth be told," George said.

"Don't give up hope yet," I said. George deserved someone special like Polly in his life, and I hated to think that might end.

"I haven't, but I am growing more worried by the day," he said. "I may have to go there myself and drag her back home someday. That's why I would welcome any tasks you might need taken care of, especially since Jake is so far away."

"Have you been keeping tabs on my boyfriend?" I asked him. The two were friends, and it wasn't all that unusual for them to talk.

"He keeps in touch," George said.

"Good. He likes you, Mr. Mayor."

George looked pleased by my statement. "I assure you, the feeling is mutual."

My cellphone rang, and when I glanced down at the caller ID, I was overjoyed when I saw that it was Jake himself. "Speak of the devil and he appears," I said as I held my phone up. "It's Jake."

"Take it," George said. "We'll chat later."

"Bye," I said as I answered my phone.

"Bye? I haven't even said hello yet," Jake said.

"I was just talking to George. How are you doing?"

"Right now, the bad guy is winning, and it's killing me," Jake said with a hint of deflation in his voice. "He's going to be tough to catch, since the only pattern I've been able to discern so far is that he's randomly murdering men named Kevin. We can't watch all of the Kevins in the area, and he's bound to strike again before we can stop him."

"Don't worry. You'll get him eventually," I said as cheerfully as I could manage.

"I'll do my best," he said, "but how many more Kevins are going to have to die first?"

"Jake, I know that I don't tell you this very often, but I can't even imagine how difficult your job must be," I said.

"Unfortunately, that's one of the results of being good at what I do. They don't call me *unless* the case is tough. Enough about me. What's this I hear about you being involved in another murder investigation?"

"How could you possibly have already heard about that?" I asked. "Did George call you? You're not keeping tabs on me, are you?"

He laughed heartily. "I know better than that. No, Chief Martin asked my help on something related, and he brought me up to speed on what you've been up to."

"Are you working on the case with him?" I asked. Jake was a crackerjack investigator, and I knew that if he were working on the chief's side, Grace and I most likely wouldn't stand a chance of bringing the killer to justice. It had nothing to do with them being men and us being women. Jake was a trained State Police Investigator, and other cops called him in when the cases were too hard for them to solve. Chief Martin was no slouch either.

"No, I'm just doing a little pro bono consulting on the side," Jake said quickly. "That's a new one on me, by the way, the victim being stabbed with a ceremonial spear."

"The method might have been a little unorthodox, but the results were just the same. I found the body, Jake," I said, letting a little of the tremor in my voice escape.

"I know, and I'm so sorry," he said. "I wish that I'd been there with you."

"It's okay," I said, feeling instantly better just talking to him. He had that effect on me, and it was one I hoped never went away. "I sincerely hope that it's something I never get used to, though."

"I know that *I* still haven't," Jake said, something that reassured me immensely. If my boyfriend wasn't inured to the sight of dead bodies in his job by now, then most likely I never would be, either, and I took a great deal of comfort in that fact. I hoped that murder *never* became that mundane to me.

"Were you just calling to say hello?" I asked him, purposely lightening my own tone.

"Is there a *better* reason that you can think of?" he asked, matching my attempt at levity.

"You could always just call to tell me that you love me," I said. "I never get tired of hearing that."

"And I don't ever tire of saying it. Suzanne, be careful. I love you."

"I love you, too, and you be careful yourself, mister," I said.

After we hung up, I realized that I suddenly felt better. Grace and I were no closer to finding Zane Dunbar's killer than we had been before, but I'd spoken with Jake, and that had been enough to take away some of the burden I'd been feeling from the murder. It was nice having him in my corner, even if he *was* clear across the state.

I still had a little time before Grace and I were due to meet up again, so I decided to pop back home and take a shower before we had lunch. Since I'd made the donuts that morning even though I hadn't sold any, I still had the scent of them on me, and while I knew that a great many men found the aroma enjoyable, I decided that, all in all, I'd rather be clean.

"Suzanne, what are you doing home so early?" Momma asked me as I walked into the cottage we shared on the edge of the park. She was at her desk in the living room going through a mound of papers. There was a fire crackling in the hearth, and soft classical music played in the background. All in all, it was exactly what a home should be, and I was happy to be a part of it.

"I didn't work the counter at the donut shop today," I

told her.

"What happened?" Momma asked, a look of concern spreading quickly across her face.

"Haven't you talked to Chief Martin today?"

"Phillip's been tied up with a fresh murder," she said. "Suzanne, tell me that you're not involved with this one, too."

"I'd like to, but I can't," I said as I kissed the top of her head. "It was Zane Dunbar from my high school class reunion."

"You never had anything to do with that boy," Momma said.

"He's hardly a boy now, not that it matters. I didn't, but it turns out that he and Grace had a history, and the two of them argued last night before he was murdered." I brought her up to date on how I'd found the body across from the donut shop, and what Grace and I had been up to since then.

After I finished, Momma nodded. "Of *course* you two have to investigate. Is there anything I can do to help?" My mother had taken Grace under her wing ever since Grace's parents had died. She considered her one of her own, which was just fine with me, since Grace was the closest thing to a sister that I'd ever have.

"We're just getting started," I said, "but thanks for the offer."

"And is Phillip being reasonable with you?" Momma asked further.

"The chief is being great," I said.

She nodded happily. "That's good to hear."

"Though I have a hunch that it's got more to do with you than with me," I said with a smile.

"Nonsense. He told me just last week that he's come to respect your ability to investigate crime."

I had to admit that it was nice that he felt that way. Grace, and even George, had contributed immensely to my investigations in the past, and I took any acclaim that

I got as praise for my team. "That's nice to know," I said.

"I still can't believe that you just shut Donut Hearts down entirely."

"I didn't," I admitted. "I made all of the donuts earlier, but Emma and her mother are still working the front. Grace and I have more work to do, so I decided to let them close up for me."

"That's still a huge step for you," Momma said. "Maybe someday you'll even find a way to take a vacation."

"Jake and I have been talking about taking a long weekend away the next time he finishes up with a case. There's a cabin in the mountains that sounds perfect."

"Then by all means, you should do it."

"I hope to, but I don't think it's going to be anytime soon. He's up to his chin in a pretty gruesome case in Wilmington."

"Do I want to know about it?" Momma asked.

"No, you're better off not hearing any of the details. Anyway, it might be awhile before he's off again. I'm not here long myself. I just wanted to pop in, take a quick shower and change my clothes, and then I'm heading out again."

"Should I make you something for lunch?" Momma asked as she started to get up.

"Thanks, but Grace and I are going to grab a bite to eat out together."

"That sounds lovely," Momma said, and I realized that she usually spent her days all alone.

"You're welcome to join us, you know," I said.

She pursed her lips, and then Momma said, "It's tempting, but I have a dozen account statements I need to go through by five this evening."

"Are you having trouble with one of your investments?" I asked her as I looked down at the stack of documents on her desk.

"I'm not sure yet. Either one of my partners has had an extraordinary run of bad luck lately, or he's stealing from me."

"And you can tell which it is just by those statements?" I asked.

"You'd be amazed what tales numbers can tell," she said. "You don't have to keep me company, or worry about me at all. I've got more than enough on my plate as it is."

"Good luck with it," I said, and then I headed upstairs. I loved my shower at the cottage, and the fact that I had the small upstairs to myself. In many ways it was like having my own suite, since no one else ever came up there unless Grace was sleeping over in the guest room next door to mine. I'd been reluctant to move back in with Momma after my divorce from Max, but it had been a blessing in disguise. We'd grown beyond the mother-daughter stage into roommates and friends, something that I cherished. Sure, she was still overprotective of me at times, but mostly we got along just great.

Twenty minutes later, I came back downstairs, washed, shampooed, and wearing clean clothes. It was almost as good as a nap, not that I had time to take even the shortest one of those. Grace would be waiting on me, and I needed to get going.

"I'll see you this evening, Momma," I said. "Do you have any plans?"

"Phillip is taking me out if he can make the time for it."

"Don't you mind being an afterthought like that?" I asked her.

"Believe me, he is most attentive normally, but I understand when he's working on a murder case that his attentions have to be divided. I'm sure that you've learned the same lesson with Jake."

"I could be wearing a nightie made of bacon, but if he's thinking about a case, he wouldn't even notice me," I said with a smile.

"And do you mind that?"

"Honestly, I've come to expect it," I said.

"As have I. Thus are the perils of dating a lawman," she said.

"I can live with it," I said.

"As can I. If we don't go out, I'll put something together for us both for dinner," she said.

"Don't go to any trouble on my account. If I get hungry, I'll just raid the fridge and the freezer. There's enough food to feed an army stored there."

"Help yourself then. I'd say to be careful, but you'd just roll your eyes, so I'll tell you happy hunting instead."

I rolled my eyes in exaggeration as I said, "Momma, you know that I'd *never* do that." After kissing her cheek, I headed back out to the Jeep. It was time to take the short drive down the road to Grace's so I could pick her up for lunch. I had a few new things to tell her since I'd seen her last, and I was really interested in getting her take on Candy.

All of those thoughts flew out of my head though, as I pulled into Grace's driveway.

She was out on her wide front porch, but she wasn't alone.

Billy Briscoe was there, and he didn't look very happy.

It appeared that I'd arrived just in time.

Chapter 7

"Billy, what's going on?" I asked him as I walked up the steps.

"Suzanne, this doesn't concern you," Billy said as he looked at me.

"Funny, but that's not really your call to make, now is it?" I glanced at Grace and asked, "Are you okay?"

"I'm fine," she said. "Billy was just leaving."

"No, Billy was not," he said. "I'm not finished with either one of you. I didn't kill Zane Dunbar, and the sooner you and the cops understand that, the better off *everyone* is going to be."

"Billy, you're not *threatening* us, are you?" I asked him innocently.

Grace, who had been looking a little unsettled before, finally smiled.

"Of course not," Billy said, trying his best to be friendly. "It's just so unnerving having people think that I'm a killer."

"Tell me about it. Since you're already here, would you mind sharing with us what you told Chief Martin earlier?" I asked.

Billy stared at me for a second, and then he shook his head and laughed as he brushed past where I stood on the steps. "I didn't come by to answer your questions," he said. "I've said my piece, and now I'm going to go."

"There's no need to rush off," Grace said with a smile, and it was good to see that she was back completely.

Billy just waved as he got into his car and drove away.

"What did I miss?" I asked Grace as I joined her on the porch.

"It seems that Billy Briscoe doesn't like being on anybody's list of suspects."

"Why? What did he say?"

"About what you'd expect," Grace answered.

"Do you think that he could be the killer?" I asked her.

"I don't know, but he hasn't done anything to take his name off the list, that's for sure. Who knows one way or the other at this point? We both know that it's pretty miserable being a murder suspect. Maybe he's just overreacting to that, not that I can blame him. It might be nothing."

"Then again, it might be something after all. Maybe we should dig a little harder into his relationship with Zane," I said as my stomach rumbled a little. "After we have lunch, of course."

"I'm kind of hungry," Grace said. "Should we walk over to the Boxcar, or should we drive?"

The day was finally warming up, and the clouds were beginning to break up. "Why don't we walk? It will give me a chance to bring you up to date on what's been happening with me since we last spoke."

Grace looked surprised by my comment. "Suzanne, we haven't been apart *that* long, and I can see that you've showered and changed. What else did you have time to do?"

"Let me tell you all about it," I said, and then I proceeded to bring her up to speed on my conversations with Candy, George, and finally, Jake.

Grace whistled softly. "Do you think Candy's smarter than she looks?"

"She puts on a good act, but the girl's not stupid, at least when it comes to manipulating people. She looks like cotton candy on the outside, but I've got a hunch that there's a jawbreaker just below the surface."

"Then we need to dig into her past with Zane, too," Grace said. "We've got a lot to do, don't we?"

"Don't worry," I said as we neared the Boxcar Grill. "We'll still have time to eat."

"That's a relief," Grace said with a smile.

"I didn't realize that you were that hungry," I said.

"I'm not, but I know how you get when *you* are," she answered with a grin.

"I'd argue the point with you, but we both know that I'd be wrong."

"Then let's go see what Trish has on the menu today, shall we?"

"After you," I said as I followed her up the steps to the converted railroad car that served as Trish's dining room. It was still relatively empty, given the fact that it was approaching eleven. There were a handful of diners already there, but Grace and I still had plenty of tables and booths to choose from. Trish was at her usual station up front by the cash register, and her face lit up when she saw us.

"Three for lunch?" she asked with a broad smile, her perennial ponytail bobbing up and down as she spoke.

"Actually, there's just the two of us," I said.

"And I make three. I'd like to join you, if you don't mind. I'm ready for a break, so you two couldn't have picked a better time." She hesitated before she answered, "Unless you need to be alone to discuss something important."

"What have you heard, Trish?" I asked her.

"A little bird came in earlier telling me that you two were looking into Zane Dunbar's murder," she explained. "I hope that wasn't supposed to be a secret."

"If it was, it's out now," I answered with a grin. "Do you mind telling me who told you?"

"I'd like to keep his identity secret, but I am willing to say that he's a cop on the force."

Most likely it was Officer Grant. There wasn't much he missed, and I had a hunch that he would make a good chief himself someday.

"That's good enough," I said. "We'd love to have you join us." I turned to Grace and asked her, "Wouldn't we?"

"We would," she agreed.

"Excellent. Do you need menus, or do you know what you want?" Trish asked.

"I feel daring. We'll have what you're having."

Trish frowned. "Are you sure? It's not on the menu, and you might not like it."

"Why not? We're feeling adventurous today," Grace said.

"Good enough. Let me go place the order, and then I'll join you. Find us a good table near the front, okay? I still have to run the register."

As we took a table front and center, Grace asked me, "What do you suppose we're having for lunch?"

"I haven't a clue. I just hope that Trish isn't on one of her crazy diets. If she is, we might be having anything." Trish was in the same boat as I was, a good fifteen pounds over my ideal weight, but she was much more aggressive about fighting it than I was. I was beginning to accept it since Jake seemed to be so pleased with me being curvy, but Trish was something else entirely. She'd go on these crazy diets for a few weeks, fall off the wagon for a month, and then she'd start something else entirely.

Maybe it was a bad thing to admit about myself, but I was hoping we were in the wagon phase where anything good and fattening was fair game.

A few minutes later, she came out carrying three identical plates, each holding a small scoop of cottage cheese, a canned pear half, and a single leaf of lettuce.

Our bad luck; we'd gotten the timing wrong.

As Trish hesitated at our table, I wanted to change my order, but I decided that if she could eat it, then so could Grace and I.

Besides, we could always sneak away later for something more substantial.

"Be right back," Trish said as she moved past us and put the plates down in front of three older women wearing brightly colored clothing.

"That was close," Grace said softly with a sigh.

"We're not out of the woods yet," I answered before Trish came back our way.

"Two minutes," she said as she passed us holding two fingers up.

I wasn't sure that was a good thing, since I doubted it would take all that long to make duplicates of the sparse meals that we'd just seen delivered.

As Trish came out of the kitchen, there was a broad smile on her face. Her tray held three cheeseburgers, heaping mounds of French fries, and chocolate shakes on the side. I didn't realize that I was holding my breath until she put the food down on our table. "I know that the milkshakes might be a little too overindulgent for the two of you," Trish said, "but I felt like a treat, and you both said that you'd try anything."

"I'm willing to make the sacrifice," I said with a grin.

"If you don't want yours, I'll take it," Grace responded with a smile of her own.

"I don't care how you divvy up *your* meals," Trish said as she sat down with us. "As long as you both keep your hands off my plate and my drink, we'll be fine."

"That's a deal," I said as I pulled my plate closer.

It was everything I'd hoped for in a lunch, and more. "Wow, I don't think I'll be able to eat again for weeks," I said.

Grace laughed.

"What's so funny?" I asked her.

"You say that all of the time, and yet you still manage to find a little room for something a few hours later."

"What can I say? I must have a speedy metabolism," I said.

Trish laughed. "You two are good for me; you know that, don't you?"

"What's going on? Are you a little down?" I asked her.

"No, I'm fine. It's just nice to see you both, that's all."

"Agreed," we said in near unison.

After we were finished, I started to pull out my wallet when Trish said, "Put your money away, Suzanne. This one was on me."

"We can't do that to you," I said.

"Sure you can," she answered.

I turned to Grace. "What should we do?"

"Listen to the lady, and then bring her a dozen donuts tomorrow."

Trish protested, "If you bring me donuts, you know that I'll just eat them."

"Good. That's what they're for," I said.

"Tell you what," Trish said. "If I let you pay, will you skip the donuts? I'm starting a new diet tomorrow, and I can't afford the temptation."

"It's a deal," I said, "but if you change your mind later, the offer is always open."

"You've got it, but I have high hopes this time," Trish said.

"You can do it," I said. "We have faith in you."

"Thanks," she said as we all approached the register.

I paid for our lunches as Grace asked, "Who said this was going to be your treat, Suzanne?"

"You're not going to fight me, too, are you?" I asked her.

"No; if you're willing to buy, I'll take it, as long as I get the next one."

"Sold," I said.

After we finished with our transaction, Trish said, "Now don't be strangers, you two."

"We wouldn't know how," I said.

After we were outside, Grace said, "Lunch was great, but I'm not sure what we should do now."

"I've got an idea," I said.

"Let's hear it," Grace replied.

"Did you notice Gary Thorpe at the reunion last night?" I asked her. Gary ran our local camera store, and I didn't know how he managed to hang on in the new digital age of cameras and photos. We'd already lost our small bookstore and our video rental place, too, and I had a hunch that Gary would be the next business in town to fall to new technology. At least no one had figured out how to make a digital copy of a donut yet, but if they ever did, I knew that I'd be sunk as well.

"Sure, I saw him a few times wandering around in the crowd," Grace acknowledged.

"And what exactly was he doing?"

Grace smiled. "He was interviewing people for the reunion with his handheld camera, and when he wasn't doing that, he was getting lots of candid shots of the crowds."

"I'm thinking that he might have something that's useful to our investigation," I said.

"That's brilliant, Suzanne. Do you think Chief Martin has thought of that yet? Should we tell him, or talk to Gary ourselves first?"

"Let's see if Gary has anything useful. If he does, we can always get a copy for the chief."

"And get one for us, too," Grace said. "I like the way that you think."

"Thanks," I said as we headed into the park toward my house. "Let's pick my Jeep up, and we can head straight over there."

"Sounds good to me," Grace said.

"You don't mind that I drive us most places these days, do you?" I asked her as we walked through the park toward home.

"No, to be honest with you, I've been glad. We've got a new accounting system in place where we have to log every mile we drive for business."

"Don't you get to use your car at all for yourself?" I asked. Grace loved her luxury company car, and she often claimed that it was one of the nicest perks of her job.

"We do, but the mileage for personal use is limited."

"I suppose you had to know that it was coming. After all, companies everywhere are starting to keep a tighter rein on expenses."

"That's the thing. This isn't coming from Corporate," Grace said. "My boss's boss is trying to make a name for herself within the organization, and this is just one of her crazy new rules. I don't think it's going to last, though."

"Why not?"

"My boss has a plan to end her reign of terror soon," she said with a smile.

"Do I want to even know more about it?" I asked.

"No, but you're lucky to be out of the corporate world. It feels as though the less there is at stake, the harder people fight about it."

"It doesn't sound like fun, but believe me, I have my own set of problems."

"I'm sure that you do," Grace said, "but at least you are your own boss."

"I am that," I said as we approached my Jeep and we got in. As I started the engine, I said, "Next stop, Gary's Camera World."

"I just hope that he's got something helpful for us," Grace said.

"You and me both," I said.

"Hey, Gary," I said as Grace and I walked into the small shop just down Springs Drive from Donut Hearts. "Do you have a second?"

"Look around," Gary said with a frown. "Do you *see* any customers?"

The store was empty, and it was hard to remember a time that it had ever been full. Gary, a paunchy man with thinning hair, looked as though he'd welcome someone coming in for change, let alone a paying customer looking for a camera, or even any accessories.

"Sorry about that," I said.

"Maybe I should close the camera shop and start making donuts," Gary said with a grin, trying to lighten his earlier tone.

"Be my guest," I said with a laugh. "You might be surprised by my razor thin profit margins on donuts, though. Surely you can come up with something better than making donuts for a living. Trust me, the hours alone will put you in an early grave."

"Okay then, maybe something else," Gary agreed. "Honestly, when I shut this place down, and it's not a question of if, it's a matter of when, I won't be starting another new business. It's too hard this day and age. No, I'm going to find a place where I can do my work, get my check at the end of the week, and have a life outside of business."

"Now you're talking fantasy," I said with a smile. "Are there any jobs *like* that?"

"I've got one," Grace piped up. "And believe me, it's wonderful."

We all laughed at that.

After a few seconds, Gary asked, "What can I do for you ladies? Are you looking for a new and extremely expensive camera, by any chance?"

"No, I'm sorry, but this isn't about cameras," I said. "We noticed you at the reunion last night taking a lot of video footage of the events."

Gary nodded. "I'm going to offer them online after I edit them. Hey, maybe I'll do *that* for a living. I could record all kinds of events and then sell them later."

"Why not?" I asked, though I didn't know the first thing about how he might go about that. "Is your footage from last night available?"

Gary frowned. "Not really. I took three hours of video, and I want to cut that down to an hour before I put it up for sale."

"We'd like to look at the uncut version," Grace said.

Gary looked intrigued by the request. "May I ask

why?"

I looked at Grace, who nodded, and then I said, "We're looking into Zane Dunbar's murder, and we thought there might be something useful somewhere in your footage. Have the police talked to you about it yet?"

"No, why, do you think they will?" Gary asked.

"Once it occurs to them, I'm sure of it," I said. "So what do you say? Can we have a look?"

"We'll be glad to pay you for a copy," Grace said.

Gary bit his lower lip, and then he asked, "How much would it be worth to you?"

"How about ten bucks?" I asked.

"Come on, I was going to ask for twenty for the finished product," Gary said. "I've got to make *something* for my work, or I'm going to have to shut this place down."

Grace pulled two twenties out of her wallet and laid them on the counter. "Forty, and that's our final offer. Take it or leave it."

"Are you sure you can't go to fifty?" he asked, though I noticed his gaze was still on the money Grace had put down.

"Any more than forty, and we'll just borrow the copy the police are going to get from you for free," she said. We both knew that there were limits to what the police chief would share with us, and that video would be way over the line.

Gary thought about it for a few seconds, and then he nodded as he grabbed the twenties before we could change our minds. "I'll be right back."

"Where are you going?" I asked him.

"I've got to save it to a zip drive," he said. "It won't take a minute."

"We want all of it, Gary. Do you understand?" Grace asked before he could duck into the backroom.

"Trust me, that's what you'll get," he said.

After he was gone, I looked at Grace. "You didn't have

to pay *that* much for it," I said.

"It's cheap at twice the price if there's anything on there that might help us prove who the murderer is, and that I'm innocent," she said.

"Could we *get* that lucky?" I asked her.

"All we can do is try," she said.

Gary was as good as his word. He came back in less than a minute carrying a small zip drive. "It's all there," he said. "Good luck."

"Thanks," Grace said.

"Gary, you might want to go ahead and make a copy for the police," I said. "I have a hunch they're going to want to see this, too."

"Why don't you give them yours when you're done with it?" he asked with a smile.

"Because we *paid* for ours," I said. "See you around."

"Bye. Thanks for stopping in, and thank you for the business."

He'd overcharged us for the footage, and what's more, we all knew it, but I hadn't said anything to chide him. I couldn't let that one go, though. "Feel free to come by and get a donut anytime. We're running a special for merchants who work along Springs Drive."

"What do I get?" he asked.

"You pay five dollars for every donut," I said.

"That sounds a little high to me," Gary said with a frown.

"Given the cost of video footage, I figured that would be well within your budget."

Gary's smile was a little sad. "Okay, if you believe that I overcharged you by that much, name your price and I'll take whatever you're willing to pay me," he said as he put the twenties back on the counter.

Grace shoved them back at him. "Forget everything that she just said, Gary. This had nothing to do with Suzanne. You named your price, and I paid it. If I'd meant to haggle with you, I would have done it *before* I paid. As far as I'm concerned, we made our deal. That money is yours. Keep it."

"Are you sure?" he asked.

"I'm positive," Grace said. "Come on, Suzanne."

After we left the camera shop, Grace asked me, "Did you *have* to get that last zinger in?"

"I didn't *have* to, but I *wanted* to, so I did," I replied. "By the way, he *did* overcharge us, whether you think so or not."

"Of *course* he overcharged us," Grace said as we got back into my Jeep. "What he didn't know was that he could have held me up for even more. I would have paid a hundred for that footage if he'd demanded it."

"I just hope that it's worth it," I said as I pulled out.

"Let's go to my place and see, shall we?" she asked.

Chapter 8

"Is there any way to watch this on a screen bigger than your notebook computer?" I asked Grace as we walked into her house. "I don't usually mind looking over your shoulder, but three hours is a long time to be squinting at a small screen."

"We don't have to worry about that, Suzanne," she said. "After I load the zip drive onto my computer, we can play it on my big-screen television. It's going to be a lot bigger than my thirteen-inch monitor."

"Cool," I said. "It sounds like it will be like watching a movie."

"Maybe one before it has been edited, without a star, a script, or any discernible plot," she said. "I'm not expecting much from Gary's rough cut."

"To be fair, though, we're looking for clues, not a cinematic experience."

"Why can't it be both?" she asked with a smile. "I'd make popcorn, but we already had lunch."

"I appreciate the thought, anyway," I said as Grace got out her computer and stuck the zip drive into it. After a minute, she tapped a few keys and then turned on her television.

In a matter of moments, I heard Gary's voice as he surveyed the outside of the school. "Here we are, back again. This is test one, test one, April Springs Multi-Year Class Reunion."

The camera showed us the event from Gary's perspective. His audio additions were scattered throughout the video, but what he lacked in dramatic storytelling skills, he more than made up for with raw footage. No one was safe from Gary's cameras, even those hiding in dark corners or outside in the shadows. First, we got a sample of his entry into the main event where the Hawaiian luau theme was everywhere. When he panned over the spears holding up the main sign, I felt a shiver go through me. One of those spears had been used to kill Zane Dunbar. I couldn't tell which one was the murder weapon and which one was blameless, and it really didn't matter, but for some reason, it really started to bother me.

"Freeze that shot," I blurted out.

The camera stayed on the banner and the spears. "Did I miss something?" Grace asked.

"Can you tell which spear killed Zane?" I asked her as I studied the frozen image.

"What? No, of course not. I never even saw the body, let alone the spear. Can you tell?"

"They look exactly the same to me," I said as I stood and got closer to the screen. The clarity was remarkable. Whatever style camera Gary used had been a good one.

"That's because I'm sure that they are identical," Grace said.

"Not quite. Don't forget, one of them killed Zane Dunbar."

"To be precise, one of them was *used* to kill Zane," Grace said. "What could it possibly matter which one was used to kill him?"

"It doesn't matter at all," I said. "Go on. Turn it on again."

"Are you sure?"

"Positive," I said, and the image with the spears quickly jumped off the screen to be replaced by a punchbowl brimming with questionable contents. "That stuff was dreadful, wasn't it? It could have peeled the paint off a car."

"I couldn't actually bring myself to taste it," Grace said. "Once I got it close to my nose, I couldn't stand the thought of actually touching it to my lips."

"I wish I'd followed your lead," I said.

"You actually drank some?"

"Just a sip, and then it went right back into my cup. It

tasted like a mix of antifreeze and frying oil."

"Suzanne, have you ever *tasted* antifreeze or frying oil, let alone the two of them mixed together?" Grace asked me.

"No, but I have a pretty vivid imagination," I countered.

"I'll give you that."

As the scene began to move again, I marveled at how the people I'd gone to high school with had changed so much over the years. One boy I'd had a huge crush on was now plain and drab, and I wondered what I'd ever seen in him. A girl I'd been friends with who'd been a little on the homely side was now a real beauty. It was as though there was no rhyme or reason to how their appearances had changed over time.

I was still marveling over that when I spotted Zane for the first time on the footage, but it wasn't his image that attracted my attention. It was the person he was speaking with.

Off to the side and out of the camera's main focus, Zane and one of our witnesses were having a heated discussion.

Why did it not surprise me all that much that it was Candy Murphy?

"I wish the sound was better on this recording," Grace said as we watched Candy and Zane in earnest conversation.

"I just hope he keeps the camera on them a little longer," I said. Gary was talking inanely about the way everyone was dancing as he focused on some classmates in the foreground of the shot. My worst fears were realized as he started to pull away, but as the image of the two of them went out of frame, I saw Candy reach out and slap Zane's face. I wished that Gary had kept on them long enough to show his expression, but the action was clear enough. What had Zane done to make her react that way? It certainly explained why Candy was so interested in the murder investigation. She was more involved in it than we'd known. The irony was that I might have missed the slap altogether if Candy hadn't approached me earlier about Zane, since the confrontation all took place in the background of another shot. I wasn't even certain that Gary had been aware of what had been happening as he'd filmed it.

Grace grabbed a pencil and started writing.

"What are you doing?"

"I'm taking notes on where things happen in the sequence so we can find them again in a hurry," she said.

"Smart thinking," I answered.

Nothing much more of note happened for another twenty-seven minutes. Some attendees got noticeably drunker over time, and the janitor, an older man with a shock of white hair, had a tough time staying ahead of the trash that the group seemed to spontaneously generate. It was all slow and painful to watch, but we were afraid to fast-forward the video for fear of missing something going on in the background. Our diligence was finally rewarded when I caught something a moment before Gary moved the camera.

"Wait," I said. "Go back."

"What did you see?" Grace asked as she did as I requested.

"I'm not sure," I said, but I had a hunch that I'd seen what I thought I'd seen. "There. Right there. Pause it."

As Grace hit the pause button, I could see in the background Janet and Billy, and it was pretty clear that they were sharing more than the dance floor. They were actually kissing.

Wow. There was more to that relationship than the freshly minted widow had been willing to admit.

"Be sure to mark the time on *that* one," I said.

As Grace jotted down a few notes, she asked me, "How did you even *see* that? I was looking at the footage, too, but I missed it completely."

"I got lucky, I guess," I said.

"We both know that it's more than that," Grace said. "I wonder what Janet will say when we show her that particular little segment?"

"Grace, it sounds as though we're blackmailing her," I said.

"No, not at all. We just found a way to encourage her to talk to us, that's all."

Grace was grinning when I glanced over at her.

"Okay, I can see that," I finally answered.

"Let's see if we can find anything else that juicy," Grace said as she started the video again.

We watched it until near the end, when Grace finally said, "I thought that I had enough of this reunion before, but seeing it all over again is almost too tough to take. Suzanne, can we stop it now?"

"You can go do something else if you need to," I said, "but I'm watching until the bitter end."

She sighed heavily, and then she replied, "No, I'll watch it, too. If you can take it, then so can I."

Ultimately I was glad that we'd both watched. During the last thirty seconds of footage, just as Grace was about to turn her computer off, we both caught something, and this time, so did Gary.

Tom Hancock could be clearly seen in the background waving a finger angrily under Zane's nose.

Gary even commented on it. "Clearly not *everyone* here tonight was happy to catch up, but for most folks, this reunion was a chance to see old friends again, and even make some new ones."

"What was that all about?" I asked her.

"I thought the closing *was* a little forced," Grace said. "If Gary's going to try to make a living doing this, he's going to have to lighten his patter a little."

"I'm not talking about the voice-over," I said. "What was Tom threatening Zane about?"

"Maybe it had something to do with the argument they had earlier."

"Maybe. I'd still like to ask Tom about it the next time we see him."

"When do you think that might be?" Grace asked as her hands went automatically to primp her hair a little.

"I say we show this to the chief, and then we go ask Tom, Janet, Billy, and Candy about what we saw on the video."

"I'm willing to bet that at least *some* of them have reasonable explanations," Grace said.

"The ones I want to talk to are the ones that don't," I replied.

"Either way, it should make for a fun afternoon."

"Can you play that on just your computer screen, or do you need a big television to show it?" I asked Grace.

"It's actually easier to view it on my computer, even if the footage isn't quite as clear as it was on the big screen."

"I guess my question is, will our suspects be able to recognize themselves on the display if it's not blown up way out of proportion?"

"Oh, yes," Grace said. "There's no doubt about it, now that we know where to look."

"Then let's go find the chief, and then we'll do some follow-up interviews."

"That sounds great to me," Grace said. "You drive. I want to copy this onto my hard drive."

"Isn't the little zip thingy enough?" I asked her.

She smiled as she explained, "Yes, the zip drive would usually be perfect, but I have a hunch the police chief is going to want a copy of his own. We watched it from the drive, but now I want one for us. It will be a lot easier to surrender the drive if we make our own backup first."

"You have an excellent criminal mind, my friend," I told Grace with a smile.

"It comes from always suspecting people's ulterior

motives, and trying to figure out what the worst-case scenarios might be and prepare for them," she answered.

"That just sounds sad."

"Maybe it is, a little," Grace said, "but it's been an important part of my career in business."

"How so?"

"Over the years, I've honed my ability to back things up and cover nearly every contingency I might run into. It's saved me more than once in the past at work, I can tell you that."

"Your work sounds pretty cutthroat," I said.

"Compared to your world filled with donuts and sprinkles, it *can* get pretty intense."

"And yet you seem to have survived it all unscathed," I answered.

"I don't know if I'd say that, but I have managed at least some level of success," she said. After she shut her laptop down and closed it, Grace said, "I'm ready if you are."

"Then let's go find the police chief and show him what we've found," I said.

"Chief, do you have a minute?" I asked when I phoned him. I wanted to spring my evidence on him in person, but in order to do that, I had to know where he was first.

"Just about that," he said. "What's going on?"

"The thing is, I can't do it over the phone. Are you in your office?"

"I will be for the next ten or fifteen minutes," he said. "Is that enough time?"

"It should be plenty," I said. I was glad that Grace had come up with the idea of marking down the times on the video where the scenes we wanted to show the chief were located. It would save us a great deal of time.

"Then get over here fast," he said, and then he hung up on me.

"That went well," Grace said after I hung up.

"He's clearly agitated about something," I said as I grabbed the zip drive. "Maybe we'll be able to cheer him up a little with what we just found."

"I'm guessing that it's a coin toss about which way it goes," Grace replied as she closed her computer and slid it into her briefcase.

"How can he be that unhappy about acquiring new evidence that he didn't have to dig up himself?"

"Suzanne, you know him better than I do. Sure, he's mellowed some over the years, but he's still not what you'd call a guy who likes warm and fuzzy hugs."

I laughed out loud at the thought of trying to corner Chief Martin and hug him. "True, but this has got to be better than that."

"I don't know, I think you're a pretty good hugger myself," Grace said with a smile.

"Right back at you. We don't have much time, so don't forget that list of times you made."

"It's right here," she said as she patted her pocket.

As we headed out the door, I said, "This is going to have to be quick, so let's not allow ourselves to get sidetracked, okay?"

"Are you saying that for your benefit, or mine?" Grace asked as we got into my Jeep.

"Both, actually," I admitted.

We made it to the police station in three minutes, just another advantage of living in a small town. Everything was always close by. The station was bustling, and as we approached the front, I told the uniformed officer behind the desk that we were there to see the chief.

"He's tied up right now, but feel free to take a seat and wait." The man barely looked up from his paperwork as he spoke to us.

"Actually, we're here at his request," I said, refusing to budge an inch from my choice real estate right in front of him.

At least he looked up at us. "And you are?"

"You're new, aren't you?" Grace asked. "I'm Grace, and this is Suzanne."

He nodded, and then picked up the phone. "Chief, a Grace and a Suzanne say they're here to see you. Okay. Got it."

"You've got two minutes," he said as he started to stand to lead us back.

"You don't have to show us the way. We've been here before," I said.

Grace paused on the other side of the desk and added, "By the way, we're not 'a' anything. Like I said before, I'm Grace, and this is Suzanne." She didn't move, nor did she smile.

"Sorry. I get it," he said.

Grace smiled brightly. "Good. I'm glad we got that settled."

I appreciated Grace standing up for us as much as anyone would, but we were on a tight timeframe. "Come on, Grace."

"Bye," she said to him as we headed to the chief's office.

"Was that really necessary?" I asked her softly.

"He needed a lesson in manners, and who am I to disregard his education?"

I smiled. "Who indeed."

My smile faded when we got to the chief's office. He was on the phone, clearly agitated, and he pointed us to the two chairs across from his desk and motioned for us to sit down. I hoped that didn't trigger another lesson from Grace, but I wasn't going to hold my breath.

When Chief Martin finally got off the phone, he snapped, "I have thirty seconds before I have to leave. I'm being called in for backup on a big bust in Union Square."

"What's going on there?" I asked.

"I'm not allowed to divulge that," he said. "What have you got for me?"

I started talking quickly, spilling out as much information as I could in a short period of time. "Gary Thorpe was taking some video at the reunion last night, and we decided that it might turn out to be valuable."

"Is it on that zip drive in your hand?" the chief asked Grace, interrupting me.

"It is, but there a few things you need to know about it," I said.

Just then, Officer Grant popped his head into the office. "Sorry to interrupt, but Chief, we've got to go, and I mean right now."

"Sorry, ladies," the chief said. "Let me have the drive and we'll get to it as soon as we can."

"But we're not finished telling you everything about it," Grace complained as she handed it to him.

"Listen, I appreciate your efforts, but this is urgent," Chief Martin said as he stood and headed toward the door.

"So is this," I said as Grace and I both stood as well.

"Not *this* urgent," the police chief said, and then he and Officer Grant were gone.

He'd laid the zip drive on his desk as soon as Grace had handed it to him.

"Should we take it with us?" she asked.

"No, leave it right where it is."

"Suzanne, we have no idea when he's even going to get around to it. He might not even check out the video at all."

"Then it's his problem. We turned the information over to him, so we've done our duty."

"We're not going to just drop it, are we?" she asked me.

"Not a chance. Just because the chief isn't going to act on what we found doesn't mean that we can't. We need to speak with Janet, Billy, Candy, and Tom."

"Then let's get cracking," she said as we walked out of the police station without a single soul noticing us.

Sometimes it was good being invisible.

Chapter 9

"Janet, it's Suzanne Hart and Grace Gauge," I announced as we knocked on her hotel room door at the Bentley Hotel. "Could we speak with you a minute?" We'd gotten her room number from the front desk. It had been surprisingly easy, and I wondered how thorough hotel security was at this place. I'd expected them to at least put up a minimal fight before handing over the information.

"Janet, are you there?" I asked as I knocked yet again.

"Try the door," Grace said.

"Grace, who leaves their hotel room unlocked?" I asked skeptically as I twisted the knob.

It was open.

The problem was that we still didn't know if Janet was there or not.

I opened the door slowly. "Janet, it's Suzanne and Grace," I called out as I took a tentative step inside.

She clearly wasn't there.

Grace was on my heels. "It's empty," I said as I turned back to her, and a moment later, she pushed past me and closed the door softly behind us.

"We can't stay long," I said. "This has to be a quick hit-and-run. The last thing we can afford to have happen is for someone to catch us in here alone. How would we even start to explain it?"

"We'll think of something if it comes up," Grace said with a grin. "In the meantime, let's start hunting for clues."

Grace started going through the drawers and the closet while I headed for the desk. That appeared to be Janet's center of activity. "The phone book's open," I told Grace.

"What section is it on?"

"Restaurants," I said as I looked closer. "Somebody circled Napoli's. Do you think it's possible that she's with Angelica and her girls right now?" Angelica DeAngelis and three of her daughters ran my favorite restaurant in Union Square, maybe even all of North Carolina. They served the most delicious Italian food that anyone could want, and every time I went, I was torn between ordering old favorites and trying something new. Jake loved the place as much as I did, and we went there whenever we could. Angelica and her daughters had become good friends to me over the years, and I cherished their friendship.

"So after we finish up here, we go visit Angelica and see who Janet's eating with. My money is on Billy Briscoe. How about you?"

"I'm not taking that bet after watching the video of the reunion," I said as I glanced at the notepad the hotel supplied by the telephone. "Grace, come look at this."

She joined me, and I handed her the pad of paper, covered with hastily scribbled notes.

After a few moments, Grace handed it back to me. "Her husband hasn't been dead twenty-four hours and she's already calling about his life insurance?"

"It *is* a little fast, isn't it?"

"Fast? It's supersonic. How did she even know who to call this soon? If I ever got married and something happened to my husband, I hope that I could at least wait a few days before I tried to collect on his life insurance policy."

"Unless you were the one to kill him," I said softly.

"Hey, you don't even know the guy," she said in mock protest. "That's no way to act. We could truly be in love."

"Grace, you haven't met him either," I said. "He doesn't exist."

"How dare you talk about my future spouse that way?" she asked with a grin as she grabbed a small notebook out of her purse.

"What are you doing?"

"I'm copying this information," she said as she jotted down the most pertinent facts. I watched her write, "$500,000.00", and then she added the phone number of the insurance agent, as well as his name.

"Did you have any luck with the rest of the room?" I asked her.

"Not particularly. Janet doesn't have a very vivid imagination when it comes to her clothing," Grace said with a shrug.

"Maybe money will improve that," I said. I felt bad joking about her being widowed so recently, but her decision to pursue a payment took away a lot of the guilt. I suspected that she and Zane had shared a tumultuous marriage based on what I'd seen at the reunion, but I hoped that there had been love in the relationship at least in the beginning.

"I doubt it. Having money doesn't mean that you suddenly acquire good taste."

"True," I said as I looked around the room. "Is there anything we've missed?"

"How can I possibly know that?" Grace asked as she looked around, too.

I was about to answer her when I heard a keycard being swiped in the lock outside.

"Hide!" I said frantically.

"Where?"

"In the bathroom," I said as I shoved Grace in ahead of me. As we closed the bathroom door, I could hear the main door to the room open.

Someone was in Janet's room.

The real question was, though, was it Janet, or had someone else gotten the same idea that we had?

I put my ear to the door to try to hear who was out there, but I didn't pick up any voices, so chances were that whoever it might have been was probably alone.

"Who is it?" Grace whispered in my ear.

"I don't know," I said softly.

"Should we hide in the shower?"

I thought about being discovered in the bathroom with Grace, and wondered if being found in the shower could possibly make things any worse.

Probably not.

"Sure, why not?" I asked.

We stepped into the tub, and then Grace quietly pulled the shower curtain shut.

"What do we do now?" she whispered.

"What *can* we do? We wait."

It felt like forever, but it couldn't have been more than three minutes. I was about to tell Grace we should see if the stranger had gone yet when we both heard someone start to open the bathroom door.

It appeared that we were about to get caught, and I didn't have the slightest hint of an idea about what excuse we could possibly use to explain what we were doing there.

I could see the door begin to open around the edge of the curtain, and I grabbed Grace's hand for moral support. At least I wasn't in there alone.

As the door started to open, I heard a woman's distant voice say, "Jenn, give me a hand next door, would you?"

"I still have to replace the towels," a woman's voice said much closer than I would have liked.

"It will just take a second," the distant voice answered.

"Fine," Jenn said, clearly a little put off by the request.

I couldn't have been happier about it myself.

Once both doors closed, I pulled the shower curtain back. "Let's go."

Grace held up, though. "How are we going to get out of here? Jenn still has to be close by."

"Unless she's watching the door, we should be fine," I said. I hurried out of the tub and into the room, with

Grace right behind me.

We were just outside of the room and back in the hallway when I noticed movement next door. Instead of running away, which was my first instinct, I turned back to the door Grace and I had just escaped through and knocked loudly. "Hello?" I asked as I turned to Grace and winked, since no one else could see me from there.

"I'm sorry, but I believe she's out," the maid who had to be Jenn explained as she popped her head out of the other room.

"Thanks. We'll catch up with her later. Have a nice day."

"You, too," she said, and then Jenn proceeded to use her universal keycard and unlocked the door we'd so recently sneaked through.

As Grace and I walked down the hall, she said, "That was a close one. Nice touch with that knock, by the way."

"What can I say? I was inspired."

"The question is, *now* what do we do?" Grace asked me.

"We really don't have any choice, do we? We have to go over to Napoli's and see what Janet is up to."

"Angelica isn't going to like us making a scene," Grace said gravely.

"I wouldn't dream of doing anything like that," I said. "As a matter of fact, we'll *both* be on our best behavior, *won't* we?" When Grace didn't answer right away, I repeated, "Right?"

"Of course," she said. "I was just thinking about something."

"That's gotten us into trouble more times in the past than I want to even consider," I said with a grin.

"Rightly so," Grace answered, "but I can't help wondering if Janet *isn't* the person who killed Zane. That insurance company call is awfully suspicious, especially since he *just* died."

"Grace, just because she's greedy doesn't necessarily mean that she's a killer," I said.

"I know, but it doesn't make her 'Wife of the Year,' either."

"I'll give you that," I said. "Maybe if we catch her off-guard, we can learn the truth about what really happened."

"I hope you're right. It would be nice to wrap this case up in a nice little bow before I have to admit to the world that I'm nothing but a common thief."

As we neared my Jeep, I said, "Grace, just because you did one stupid thing when you were young doesn't mean that's who you are."

"Do you honestly believe that, or are you just trying to make me feel better?" she asked me, the hope strong in her voice.

"I believe it with all of my heart," I said.

"Thanks, Suzanne. How do you always know exactly what to say to make me feel better?"

"I believe it comes from being your best friend since before we could talk," I said with a smile.

"Maybe there's something to that," Grace said.

At least we were already in Union Square, so the drive to Napoli's wasn't all that bad. As I pulled into a parking space, I remembered the first time I'd eaten there with Jake. Someone had done a number on his car that night, but even that hadn't ruined our special night together. We'd been through a great deal since then, but it had all just managed to bring us closer together. I missed him when he was gone working on a case, but no matter where he was, a part of him was still always with me.

"Hey, who's that over there?" Grace asked as she pointed to two people arguing in the parking lot.

"One of them is Janet, but I can't tell who she's fighting with," I said as I got closer.

And then the man turned, and I saw who it was. I'd been expecting to find Billy Briscoe there with her, but I was shocked to see that it was Tom Hancock instead.

"It's Tom," Grace said.

"I know. Should I pull right next to them, or should we try to be stealthy and eavesdrop?"

"I don't think they've seen you yet, so I choose stealthy. Pull into that spot."

I did as she asked and then I quietly opened the door so that I could hear better. I didn't have much luck making out their argument. "What are they fighting about?" I asked Grace.

"I don't know, but I'm going to find out," she said as she opened her own door. Instead of sitting there listening to them, though, she actually got out.

"Where are you going?"

"Suzanne, I need to hear this," she said.

I had no choice but to follow her lead.

When we got within two rows of them, Grace moved behind a panel van that completely hid her from view. I joined her, and we began to listen in.

"I don't owe you anything," Tom said loudly. "I met you here as a courtesy, Janet, but that's as far as it goes."

"I know what my husband told me," she said angrily.

"Your husband probably said a lot of things," Tom replied coldly. "How much of it was the truth was another thing altogether."

"Are you calling him a liar?" she asked in a tone that clearly should have warned Tom off.

It didn't. "That's exactly what I'm saying," he said. "And until you can produce an IOU with my signature on it or something just as concrete, I'm done having this conversation with you."

That's when Janet lashed out at him, slapping his face so hard we could hear the impact from where we stood. When she started to slap him again, Tom blocked the strike and grabbed her arm instead.

"Let go of me," she protested.

"Not until you settle down," Tom said. He was clearly

angry, but being slapped would do that to just about anyone.

I noticed movement beside me as I saw Grace stand and start toward them.

"Where are you going?" I asked her softly but urgently.

"I've got to stop this right now before it escalates out of control," Grace said.

I had no choice at that point.

I followed her.

"What are you two doing here?" Tom asked angrily as he spotted us approaching. "Have you been following me around?" It was significant in my mind that he still had a firm grip of Janet's arm.

"We eat, too," I said before Grace could answer. "What are *you* two doing here?"

"She invited me here to eat so that she could ambush me," Tom said.

"Let go of me," Janet cried out, acting a little for our benefit, no doubt.

Tom seemed almost surprised that he still held Janet's arm. He loosened his grip, and she jerked her arm away from him.

As she rubbed her bicep, she asked, "Is that the way you treat every woman you meet?"

"Just the ones who slap me," Tom said. There was an angry white splotch on his face from where she'd connected, and I wondered how long it would take before it turned red. "Deny it. I dare you."

"I won't," she said angrily, "and I'd do it again. You tried to malign my late husband's character, and I won't stand for it."

"What's going on out here?" I heard a familiar voice ask as I struggled for some way to end this argument. It appeared that someone else was about to do it for me. Angelica DeAngelis, a dear friend of mine, the mother of four beautiful daughters and the owner of Napoli's, approached us all, wielding a French rolling pin as though it were a weapon, which in her hands, it clearly was.

"It's nothing," I said quickly.

"That's exactly what it's not," Angelica said angrily. "Two customers just complained about an argument in my parking lot." She turned to Janet and Tom. "When I asked you to leave my restaurant before because of your argument, I expected you both to leave the premises. I've already banned you from coming back to Napoli's. Do I need to call the police as well?" She turned to Grace and me then. "I'm surprised to find you both here. Are you two a part of this?"

"We just got here," I said quickly.

"We were trying to make the peace," Grace added.

Angelica looked a little mollified by the news. "And have you had any success?"

"Not so far," I said with a shrug. I couldn't afford to get banished from the restaurant. Not being able to eat at Napoli's whenever the mood struck me would be devastating.

"Then I will take care of it myself," Angelica said as she pulled out her cellphone.

Tom was the first to back down. "You don't have to call the police on my account. I was leaving anyway." He gave Janet one last cold glare, and then he said to her, "Go ahead and sue me. I will welcome the opportunity to let everyone know what really happened between your husband and me. Just be prepared to learn some pretty unsettling things about the man you were married to for all those years."

"Don't push me," Janet said, "or I will come after you with all that I've got."

Tom didn't even look in our direction as he stormed off to his car, and Angelica headed back inside, but not before nodding in my direction. At least we were still okay.

For the moment.

"Thanks for trying to protect me from him," Janet said to Grace and me after Angelica was gone.

"I'm sorry; is that what you thought just happened here?" Grace asked.

Janet looked confused by her question. "Do you mean that it wasn't?"

"Make no mistake about it. We want to find out who murdered your husband," I said. "That's *all* that we're interested in at this moment in time."

"Then you should go after Tom Hancock," she said angrily. "Now that Zane's dead, he won't have to pay back *any* of the money he stole from us."

"Can you prove any of that?" I asked her.

"Not yet, but believe me, I will, even if it takes my last breath to do it, and every last dime I have to my name," Janet vowed.

"That's going to be considerably more when you cash in your husband's life insurance policy, won't it?" Grace asked her.

"What makes you think that he even *had* life insurance?" Janet asked.

"Come on, don't try to act dumb," Grace said. "You have half a million dollars coming your way."

"How did you find out about that? That's supposed to be confidential information," Janet snapped.

"Funny how that works sometimes," I said. "We know more than you could ever believe."

Was it my imagination, or did Janet's pupils dilate when she heard me say that? "I'm just getting what I'm entitled to. After all, Zane paid those premiums for years to look out for me after he was gone. Why shouldn't I get what's coming to me?"

"I hope that's exactly what happens, that you get *everything* that you deserve," Grace said. It was obvious that she hadn't meant it in a good way at all.

"Janet, don't you think calling your agent the day your husband's body was discovered might be considered a bit premature in some people's point of view?" I asked.

"I can't survive without it," Janet said. "Zane and I had obligations that won't stop just because he's gone."

"Like what, for example?" Grace asked her.

"Car payments, house payments, premiums, things like that," she said. Janet looked around the parking lot and then she added, "I don't need to stand here answering your questions. I'm going back to my hotel."

"Would you like us to go with you?" Grace asked.

Janet looked surprised by the suggestion. "Why would I want that?"

"We could offer you comfort," I suggested.

"I don't think so," Janet said, and then she was gone.

"That went well, didn't it?" Grace asked me once she was gone.

"It could have gone a great deal worse," I said as I started toward the back door of the restaurant.

"Are we going to eat at a time like this?" Grace asked as she followed me.

"First of all, I'd eat Angelica's food anytime I have the chance, but that's not why I'm going to the restaurant."

"If you're not going in to eat, then why are you going?"

"I want to hear more about the fight that got Janet and Tom banned from Napoli's," I said. "Can you imagine anything worse happening?"

"Well, being murdered is pretty bad, and there a few things that are near that, but overall, no, it's nothing that I ever want to have happen to me."

"Then let's go see if Angelica or one of her daughters has anything to add to our investigation," I said as I knocked on the restaurant's back door.

Chapter 10

"Come in," Angelica said after we knocked on the kitchen door. She looked toward the parking lot and asked, "Are your friends gone?"

"They both took off, but they aren't really our friends," I said. "What happened in the restaurant?"

"All I know is that Maria came to get me when they were making a fuss at the table. You should talk to her to get the full story."

I looked around the kitchen, but none of Angelica's daughters were there. That was odd, since I knew that they shared in the duties of Napoli's, including the cooking. "Where is she?"

"She's taking care of some customers, but she'll be in shortly. Sophia's helping her, not that she needs it, but my youngest daughter needed a break from her mother, so I approved it."

"And Antonia?" I asked.

"She's visiting Tianna," Angelica said. There had been a rift between Angelica's oldest daughter and the rest of the clan, so this was good news.

"How is she doing?" I asked delicately.

"We are *all* making an effort," Angelica said, and then she clearly wanted to change to subject. "Are you two hungry?"

"We've already had lunch, and it's a little early for dinner, if that's what you're asking," I said.

"That wasn't my question," she said with a smile. "Sit. Let me put a few plates together for you."

"Honestly, we just wanted to talk to Maria," I said.

Angelica frowned at me. "What's wrong, Suzanne? You don't like my cooking anymore?"

"Hardly," I said. "I just don't know that I can afford to put on any more weight."

"Nonsense," Angelica said with a huge smile as she studied us. "You're *both* too skinny."

"Now I *know* you're lying," I said, matching her grin with one of my own. "Grace, aren't you going to take my side?"

"Speak for yourself," Grace said. "When a master chef offers to feed me, the only answer you'll ever get out of me is thank you very much."

"That's my girl," Angelica said as she pinched Grace's cheek.

"Traitor," I said playfully to Grace as the restaurant owner grabbed two plates and started filling them with abundant samples of spaghetti, ravioli, and ziti.

"Every single time," Grace said.

As Angelica brought us our plates and put them on the small table in the kitchen, she said, "Now, a little wine will round everything out perfectly."

"Just a little, though," I said.

"Absolutely," Angelica replied as she headed for their wine cupboard.

"We're never getting out of here. You know that, don't you?" I asked Grace.

"We will eventually, but in the meantime, let's just enjoy this, okay?"

I looked at the plate in front of me, amazed at how Angelica could take the same basic ingredients and make them into such different and delightful meals. The ziti had a blend of cheeses that danced across my taste buds, while the spaghetti sported a tomato-based sauce that was richly satisfying. The ravioli was stuffed with different cheeses, and the sauce she'd chosen for it complemented it perfectly. I was still sampling each individual flavor when Angelica emerged with a bottle of wine.

"I hope it's nothing too special," I said as she uncorked the bottle.

"It's just a little house wine I like myself," she said.

Grace, who knew a great deal more about wine than I

did, studied the label. "It's a lot more than that, and we both know it."

Angelica winked at her as she poured three glasses. "Shh." As she picked up her own glass, Angelica asked, "To what should we toast?"

I said without hesitation, "To family: both here and far away, but most important of all, those long gone but never forgotten."

"To family," we all repeated as we clinked our glasses together.

The wine was superb, even though I didn't know just how special it was. A few minutes after we dug into our food, the kitchen door from the dining room swung open. I was expecting to see Maria, but Sophia came in instead.

The young woman smiled when she saw us. "When did you two sneak in?"

"While you weren't looking," I answered with a grin. "How's it going out there? Is there any chance Maria might be able to spare us a minute?"

"I don't know about that. We're in the middle of a sudden rush," Sophia said, and then she turned to her mother. "I honestly don't think I can work back here anymore today."

"That's fine with me," Angelica said as she winked at us. "Help your sister."

"Hang on a second," Angelica's youngest daughter said. "That was *way* too easy. You're not trying to get rid of me, are you?"

"Sophia, you know that you're *always* welcome in my kitchen. I just don't want Maria to be overwhelmed."

"Well, okay, then," Sophia said as she grabbed an order and left.

Once she was gone, Angelica grinned at us. "That girl thinks she's so clever, but you mark my words. She'll be back here in her apron beside me in half an hour or less. She's a natural in the kitchen these days, and the others better watch out, or she'll surpass them all."

"That's high praise coming from you," I said.

"It's merited," she said.

"If they're so busy out front, should we come back later and talk to Maria?" I asked her as I cleaned my plate. How had that happened? I hadn't been hungry when I'd started, but I'd still managed to eat everything Angelica had given me. At least Grace's plate was empty, too.

"No, I'll get her for you," Angelica said as she headed for the dining room door.

"Don't pull her out of the dining room on our account," I said.

"Nonsense. My youngest was just exaggerating before."

The restaurant owner came back a minute later with Maria in tow.

"Hey, Maria. Can you spare us a minute?" I asked her.

"Glad to. Soph's got it covered up front."

"Excellent. What happened earlier?" I asked.

"The argument? It wasn't as dramatic as my dear sweet mother must have made it sound. She loves a good story more than just about anyone I know."

"It was no story," Angelica protested. "They were fighting loud enough for me to hear them all the way in here."

"Really?" Maria asked with a smile. "Then what were they fighting about?"

Angelica frowned. "Maybe I couldn't make out their exact words, but their tone was clear enough."

Maria nodded. "You're right there."

"So why *were* Janet and Tom fighting?" I asked.

"Was that their names? All I knew was that the woman claimed that the man owed her husband money, but he kept denying it."

"Did either one of them mention an amount?"

"Twenty thousand dollars," Maria said.

"That's a lot of money," I said after whistling softly under my breath.

"Some people might believe that it was enough to make it worth killing someone over," Grace added.

"I *never* understood why someone would kill for money," Angelica said. "Passion I get, but never money. It's too easily gained and lost to matter all that much to me."

"Spoken as someone who *has* money," Maria said.

Angelica turned to her. "We aren't rich, not by any means, but we have enough to live on, enough to keep this restaurant open, and enough for a few indulgences every now and then. How much more than that do we really need, when we all have each other?"

Maria smiled as she hugged her mother. "You're right," she said.

"I know that, but it's still nice to hear every now and then," Angelica said with a smile.

So far, we hadn't gotten anything new but an amount we hadn't heard before. While twenty grand was a lot of money, it still didn't seem like enough to make murder worthwhile to me.

Unless Tom owed it to Zane and didn't have it.

"Is there anything else you can remember about their time here?" I asked Maria. "Don't worry if it doesn't seem important to you. We're looking for *anything* that might help us solve a murder."

Maria frowned, and then after a moment, she said, "It's probably nothing, but she did say something that I thought was kind of strange."

"What's that?" I asked eagerly.

"Janet told him that a certain someone from his past wouldn't like it if she found out the truth about him, and that any hope he had of rekindling an old flame would be snuffed out like a candle in a hurricane. Does that mean anything to you?"

Grace looked uncomfortable with the reference, since we both figured that it had to be about her. "Maybe," I said. "Is that all?"

"That's it," she said. "Sorry I couldn't be of any more help. Now, if you don't mind, I'd better get back out front."

"Go," I said, "and thanks."

"For what it was worth," Maria said, and then she left.

"Did that help at all?" Angelica asked when it was just the three of us again.

"We never know," I said. "Thanks for the meal," I added as I kissed her cheek and hugged her, with Grace close behind me.

"It was nothing," Angelica said warmly. "Remember, I'm always here if you need me."

"We know it, and we count on it," I said.

After Grace and I were back at my Jeep in the parking lot, she asked, "How does Janet even *know* that Tom and I spent a little time together at the reunion?"

"Everybody there was commenting on how natural you two looked together out on the dance floor," I said.

"Well, that's never going to happen now," Grace said.

"Why is that?" I asked.

"The fact that he's a murder suspect might have something to do with it," Grace said.

"I meant besides that," I said.

"I don't know. Even if it turns out that Tom is innocent, I think that maybe we had our chance a long time ago, and now it's gone."

"I wouldn't discount him that quickly," I said.

"Suzanne, could we possibly change the subject?" Grace said. "I'd really like to track down the murderer as soon as we can. How about you?"

"I couldn't agree more," I said. "Is there anything else you'd like to cover in Union Square while we're here? I have an idea about something we can do back in April Springs, but if we can save ourselves a trip back here later, I'm willing to do that first."

"I'd like to talk to Billy again," she said. "I've got a

hunch there's something he's not telling us."

"Any idea what that might be?" I asked.

"No, it's just a guess at this point," she replied, "but I still think that it's worth a shot."

"I agree," I said.

As we drove to the hotel, Grace asked me, "What's your idea?"

"I want to follow that spear," I said. "I keep thinking that it wouldn't be an easy thing to remove from the gym, not to mention carry down the street to my donut shop."

"They were never actually at Donut Hearts, remember?"

"They were across the street," I said, "and that's close enough to make it personal."

"I totally get that," Grace said. "Let's tackle Billy, and then we can go digging around at the gym."

"It almost sounds as though we have an actual plan," I said with a grin.

"You never know. Stranger things have happened," Grace answered.

We were close to the Bentley Hotel when my cellphone rang. Could it be Jake? No, when I checked the caller ID, it was a surprise. What could Maria DeAngelis possibly want with me?

"Hey, Maria," I said as I answered. "It's been awhile since we chatted last."

"Suzanne, this might be nothing, but I thought you should know what just happened."

"Go ahead," I said. "I'm listening."

"Well, I was cleaning up the table where your two friends were eating, and I found a torn piece of stationery from the Bentley Hotel under the table."

This could be the development we'd been hoping for. "Did it say anything?"

"No, nothing was on it but one long number."

"That's odd," I said.

"That's not the strangest part. Thirty seconds after I found it, Janet came rushing back into the restaurant. I told her that she couldn't be there and then I reminded her that she'd been banned, but she didn't care. She said that she lost something that she *had* to get back. She sounded pretty desperate, and when I tried to get her to leave, she started getting hysterical."

"What did you do?"

"I didn't think it was all that important," Maria said, "so I showed her the paper I'd found. She grabbed it out of my hand as though it were made of gold, and then she tore out of the restaurant without another word. At first I was just happy she left before my mother threw the woman out, but now I'm starting to wonder if I should have turned it over to her or saved it for you instead."

"You did fine," I said. "Is there any chance you remembered the number?"

Maria laughed. "If it had been a name or even a note, I wouldn't have paid much attention to it, but I've always had this weird thing about numbers. They stick in my head. It was 3205. Does that mean anything to you?"

"Not right offhand," I said.

She sounded deflated as she answered, "That's too bad. I was kind of hoping that I'd found a clue."

"You might have," I said. "I just don't know what it means yet."

"Well, let me know if you ever figure it out. It's going to drive me crazy not knowing."

"That makes two of us," I said. "Thanks for calling."

"You're welcome."

After I hung up, I told Grace about the number, and Janet's reaction to losing it. "What do you think it means?" I asked her.

"It can't be a room number at the hotel," she said. "They don't go up that high."

"Well, there aren't enough digits for it to be a phone number. Could it be an address maybe?" I asked.

"What address around here is four digits long?" Grace asked me after a moment's pause.

"Sometimes people ask for verification of your social security number," I said. "That's four digits."

"It could be the second part of a phone number after all," Grace said as she took out her cellphone.

After getting a wrong number, she put her phone back in her purse. "Well, that was a dead end."

"Who did you call?"

"The prefix for April Springs, and then 3205," she said. "It was for a pizza place."

"It was still a good idea," I answered, trying to offer her some consolation. I knew how frustrating it could be when I misinterpreted a clue.

"So what else could it mean?"

"I have no idea," I said, "but I think we should ask Janet about it the next time that we see her."

"Then again, maybe we shouldn't tip her off that we even know about it just yet," Grace said. "We might be able to use the information to our advantage, but if we tell her that we know that number, it might warn her that we're on to her."

"Are we still thinking that she might have killed her husband?" I asked Grace.

"I'm not willing to say that just yet, but she *did* call that insurance agent the day her husband's body was discovered," Grace said.

"Yeah, that doesn't look too good, does it?"

"It's not exactly a character endorsement," Grace said. "In fact, it sounded pretty cold to me."

"It did to me, too," I said as I parked in the visitor's lot at the hotel.

"How should we approach Billy this time?" Grace asked me.

"Well, he wasn't exactly thrilled with us the last time we spoke. I think it's time we just come out and tell him the truth."

"What, that we suspect him of murder?"

"No, nothing that obvious. I was just thinking that maybe we should admit that we're trying to solve Zane's murder, and then see what he has to say."

"The truth's *always* worth a shot as a last resort," Grace said with a shrug.

"Then that's what we'll try, because otherwise, I'm running out of ideas."

Chapter 11

When we got to Billy's room, we could hear voices coming from inside. It wasn't that the doors were that thin, though. Whoever was in there was shouting, and they clearly didn't care *who* heard them. Grace was about to knock when I grabbed her hand.

"Let's just listen in a little first," I said.

She frowned, and then we both put our heads closer to the door. If someone came by, it would be pretty clear what we were doing, but I was willing to take that gamble.

"I don't care what you do, Billy Briscoe. As of right now, I'm done with you." It was clearly Janet's voice, and she was angry.

"I just asked you who you had lunch with," Billy said with a whine. "I'm *not* being over-possessive."

Janet's voice got louder, and I had to wonder if it was because she was now closer to the door. "I don't care. Don't call me, and don't come see me anymore. Do you understand?"

"Give me another chance, Janet," Billy pled, and I thought I could hear him start to cry.

"No," she said coldly, clearly unmoved by the display.

I glanced down to see the doorknob start to move.

Grabbing Grace's arm, I pulled her to a nearby alcove where the ice machine and a few vending machines were located.

"What are you doing?" Grace asked me.

"Shh," I said. "She's coming."

Sure enough, we heard the door slam, and a few seconds later, Janet's angry steps echoed down the hallway toward us. If she happened to glance into the alcove, Grace and I were dead, maybe even literally.

Fortunately, she passed right by us without a single

glance our way.

"Whew, that was close," Grace said after Janet was gone. "What should we do, follow her, or go talk to Billy?"

"I don't think we'll get much out of Janet when she's that mad," I said. "Besides, Billy might be a little more willing to talk to us now that he's out of the picture with Janet." Grace frowned, so I asked her, "What's wrong with that plan?"

"It seems kind of heartless going after him when his heart is breaking," she said.

"Ordinarily I would agree with you, but we can't forget that he was seeing a married woman, and he might even have had something to do with Zane's murder. We can't *afford* to tiptoe around Billy right now."

"I know you're right," she said, "but I'm beginning to wonder when we got so heartless about all of this. We didn't used to be this way."

I stopped dead in my tracks and thought about what she'd said. After a few moments, I answered, "Grace, I know you're right, but I'm not sure what to do about it. Maybe investigating all of these murders has had an impact on me after all, as much as I like to think that I'm above all that. Then again, I know that the old me would never take advantage of someone's pain, no matter how they got it. We've met too many murderers since we first started doing this. A lot of them have looked us straight in the eye and proclaimed their innocence, and some of the time I actually believed them. What we have to focus on right now is the fact that someone was murdered, and we're trying to discover who did it. If that makes us cold and calculating, then maybe it's just part of what we've both become."

"Maybe, but we're *still* human," Grace said. "As much as I love tracking down killers with you, I'm not thrilled by the idea that I'm walling off a part of me that I actually like."

"Neither am I," I said. "I don't know what we can do about it, though, do you?"

"Suzanne, I *know* that we have to keep pushing forward. I just want us to be aware of what we're doing, that's all."

"I agree," I said. "In the end, if Billy turns out to be the killer, then we were justified in grilling him."

"And if he's not?" Grace asked.

"Then we'll probably owe him an apology," I said. "With donuts."

Grace nodded and offered me a slight smile. "Sorry. I didn't mean to make an issue of it."

I hugged her. "That's one of the reasons that you're my best friend," I said. "You keep me in line when I need it."

"Right back at you," Grace said.

"Are you ready to do this?"

"I'm ready," she said, and we approached Billy's door together. I knew that I could get too caught up in our investigations sometimes, and I'd lost a few friends over the years since Grace and I had become unofficial murder investigators, but I was going to make a concerted effort to remember that many of these people were my friends, and nearly all of them deserved the benefit of our doubt. That might mean that we tiptoed a little more in the future than we had in the past, but I could live with that. In the end, I had to live in April Springs, and even the surrounding communities, and I had a business to run. I'd hate to solve a few murders and end up losing the donut shop because people didn't want to come in anymore. After all, I didn't offer anything that was essential to *anyone's* wellbeing. I was, first and foremost, a donut maker, by trade and by avocation, and if I lost that, I'd lose a very real part of myself.

"Billy, do you have a second?" I asked as I tapped on his door.

There was no answer.

I tried again, saying, "We just saw Janet leave your room, so we know that you're in there. We're so sorry about what happened."

I could hear footsteps approach the door, and then Billy opened it tentatively. He'd been crying; that much was clear from his bloodshot eyes and his runny nose. "Sorry. I've got allergies," he said as he dabbed at his cheeks with a tissue.

"I get them sometimes myself," Grace said softly. "Do you have a minute?"

"Why not?" He stepped aside and ushered us in. If I'd been alone, I would have tried to maneuver him to somewhere more public, but since Grace was with me, I felt a little safer. After all, no matter how we might sympathize with him, Billy was still a suspect on our list of possible murderers, and we'd found nothing so far to clear his name from it.

"What did she say to you?" Billy asked as he closed the door behind me. "Did she mention me?"

"No, but then again, she looked pretty upset," I said.

Billy nodded sadly. "I pushed her too hard. I know that now."

"What exactly happened, Billy?" Grace asked him.

"I don't want to talk about it," Billy said, and then he frowned at both of us. "Why are you here?"

"We're digging into Zane's murder," I said.

He looked at us as though he didn't believe us. "Since when did you two become cops?"

"We aren't," I said quickly, "but we've helped the police chief out in the past on several occasions, and he's come to rely on our assistance." That last bit was more than a little bit of a stretch, but how could Billy possibly know just how much I was exaggerating the situation?

"And you think I did it," Billy said. "Well, you're both dead wrong. I didn't kill Zane."

"You have to admit that it looks bad for you," I said.

"What are you talking about?" Billy asked, a wary edge creeping into his voice.

"Come on," Grace said. "You were seen arguing with the man a few hours before he was murdered. That doesn't exactly help your case."

"So we had a fight."

"What was it about?" I asked him. "Did it concern Janet?"

"Actually, it was about Helen Marston," Billy said.

"What *about* Helen?" I asked.

"Zane was bullying her about something at the reunion. I overheard them, and then I scolded Zane for doing it. He told me to mind my own business, and that was when the argument started."

"So you two fought over Helen," I said.

"Sure, but it could have been for any one of a dozen different reasons. Zane and I used to fight all the time in school. It's the relationship we had. Why was *this* time any different?"

"Well, for one thing, you're both grown men now," I said, "and for another, he died soon afterward, remember? Add your relationship with the widow into the mix, and I'm a little surprised that you're not sitting in a jail cell right now."

"Janet and I are just friends," Billy said, and then he added softly, "I'm not even sure we're still that at this point."

"You're more than that, and we all know it. We saw you two at the reunion," I said, keeping the fact that it was all caught on video to myself for now. "There's no use denying it."

"Nothing happened," Billy said. "I was drunk, and I tried to kiss her on the dance floor. She let me for about five seconds before she jerked away, slapped my face, and then stormed off. Did you happen to see that part of it? You're wasting your time trying to pin this on me. If you're really looking for Zane's killer, you should talk to

Mr. Davidson. He's the one who had a real motive to kill Zane."

"What might that be?" Grace asked.

"No way am I telling you that," Billy said. "If you want to know, you're going to have to get that from him yourself."

"At least give us a hint," I suggested.

Billy thought about that, and then he shrugged. "Sure, what could it hurt? Ask him about Zane and his new girlfriend."

"Zane had a girlfriend on the side?" I asked.

"Not *his* girlfriend, though I wouldn't be surprised if that were true, too. The man was a dog. I'm talking about Helen Martson." Billy was clearly expecting us to be surprised by the news, but we disappointed him. "You knew about that already, didn't you?"

"We did," I said.

"Well, you might know that, but I'm willing to bet that you *don't* know about the relationship between Helen and Zane."

"Tell us," Grace asked.

"I really shouldn't. I've said too much already," Billy said.

"We'll keep your name out of it," I promised him. "You can trust us."

He was about to add something when his cellphone rang. After a quick glance at the caller ID, he said breathlessly, "I have to take this." Grace and I stood firm as he answered his call. "Hang on one second," he said as he answered it, and then he held the phone to his chest. "Please? This might be my last chance." He was pleading now, and there was no doubt in my mind that Janet was the one on the other end of the line.

"We're going. Thanks for your time," Grace said.

"And the information," I added.

He led us out, but before he closed the door, Billy said, "Remember, you didn't hear any of that from me. You promised."

"We promised," I echoed the sentiment, and then he closed the door and deadbolted it.

"Well, that was productive," Grace said once we were out in the hallway alone. "Who do you suppose was on the other end of that telephone call?"

"Is there any doubt in your mind? It had to be Janet," I said.

"After the way she stormed out of his room after yelling at him? Do you really think so?"

"I have a hunch that Janet may have suddenly realized that she couldn't afford to have Billy as an enemy while the police are looking into her husband's murder."

"Not to mention us," Grace added.

"So far, we haven't been much of a threat," I said. "And don't tell me that these things take time. I know that, but it still frustrates me."

"It frustrates both of us," she said, "but we can only do what we can do."

"True enough," I said, "but what do we do now?"

"We don't have much choice, do we? We have to talk to Helen and see what Billy was talking about."

"Do you think that *she* might have killed Zane?" I asked as we headed back to my Jeep.

"At this point I'm not sure of anyone that we can clear," she said. "How about you?"

"Everywhere I look, I see people who wanted to see Zane out of the picture," I answered. "It must have been a tough way to live his life."

"He still deserved better than he got," Grace said.

"That's one of the reasons that I keep pushing," I said. "I'll be honest with you, though. The main thing that motivates me right now is solving this before your earlier indiscretion comes to light. I don't want you to take any hits that you don't deserve."

"I stole," Grace said softly. "I deserve whatever I get."

"What you deserve is compassion," I said tenderly.

"Once this is all over, we'll figure out a way to make this right."

"I don't know how that's possible," she said. "Everyone I wronged is gone."

"We'll come up with something. Trust me," I answered.

"I always have, and I always will," she replied.

It was a somber drive back to April Springs, and I struggled to keep myself from speeding to get there quicker. I wanted to talk to Helen Marston, and the sooner, the better.

"Helen, do you have a second?" I asked her as we walked into the office at the high school. She was a guidance counselor there, which may have explained how she'd gotten involved with one of our former teachers. I'd read somewhere that proximity in the workplace was the number one reason couples got together, and in a way, I suppose that's how Jake and I had met. The only difference was that he had been investigating a murder at the time, and I was one of his suspects.

Helen frowned before she spoke. "Sorry, but I have a meeting with a parent in three minutes."

The secretary behind the desk piped up at that point and said, "Mrs. Porter canceled. Didn't you get my email?"

"I haven't had a chance to read it yet," Helen said testily.

"Listen, we can talk out here, or we can do it in your office," I said. "Personally, I'm fine with it either way. I just thought you might want to have a little privacy for this particular conversation."

We all glanced over at the secretary as I said it, and she looked quickly away. It was pretty clear that she'd been eavesdropping on our conversation, and just as obvious that Helen wasn't pleased about it. "I suppose that would be best," she said before turning to the secretary.

"Marcy, call me in ten minutes. I have to get my notes

ready for the meeting tonight."

"Sure thing," Marcy said, and we followed Helen into her office. She took her chair behind a large dark oak desk, a commanding presence that was not so subtle about telling visitors who was in charge, at least in that particular room. It didn't faze me a bit, but I was willing to bet that it intimidated most of the students who sat where I was sitting now.

"Now, what can I do for you?" she asked as she shuffled a few papers on her desk.

"For one thing, you can tell us exactly what your relationship was with Zane Dunbar and Billy Briscoe," Grace said before I even had a chance to come up with a question. I didn't mind; I might have taken five minutes trying to work myself up to that question, but Grace had cut straight to the point.

"They were classmates of mine, the same as they were with you both," she said.

"That's not what we heard," I said. "Come on, Helen. You might as well be candid with us."

"I really don't see why I should be," she said. "You've got no cause to accuse me of anything."

"Hang on a second," I said. "No one's made any accusations, at least not yet. We're just gathering facts. We know that Billy got into an argument with Zane because of your honor last night. What exactly was *that* all about?"

Helen frowned. "Billy Briscoe has had a crush on me for years," she said. "When I started seeing Henry, he took it personally."

"I thought he had a thing for Janet," Grace said.

"That was old news," Helen said dismissively.

That wasn't what the video had shown, but I decided not to bring that up at the moment. "So Billy had a crush on you. That would explain why he might be jealous of Henry, but not of Zane," I said.

After a few moments, she sighed. "You're going to

make me say it, aren't you?"

I didn't have a clue what she was talking about. "It would be better all around if you did," I said, trying to sound as though I knew more than I was letting on.

"Fine, I'll say it. In a moment of weakness last month, I spent the night with Zane at a motel. It was a mistake, and we both knew it the next morning. I'd had a fight with Henry, and Zane had argued with Janet. We ended up at the same restaurant, and one thing led to another."

"Did anyone else know about it?" Grace asked.

"Billy spotted us coming out of the motel room the next morning," she admitted. "Listen, I'm not proud of what I did, but nobody took advantage of me."

"How did Henry and Janet react to the news?" I asked.

She looked surprised by my question. "They don't know, not unless Billy said something to them, and I'd appreciate it if you'd keep what I just told you in confidence. I could lose more than my job if word got out about what happened."

"We won't say anything unless it becomes pertinent in catching the murderer," I said.

"Why would that matter?" she asked.

"If you didn't do it, or Zane wasn't murdered because of your direct actions, then we won't tell anyone else," I said.

She was clearly shocked by my conditions. "Do you honestly think that Zane was killed because of our little indiscretion?"

I'd gotten divorced over that same type of "little indiscretion." How could she not take it more seriously than that? "It's entirely possible," I said.

"You are both looking at the wrong people as suspects," she said curtly.

"Then tell us who we should be focusing on instead," Grace said.

Helen bit her lip, and I could see the girl she'd been back in school for just a moment. She had been pretty back then in a pouty kind of way, but a lot of that had faded since we'd all left school. After a moment more, she said, "I'm going to regret this, but I can't have you stirring up trouble in my life when I'm just getting everything sorted out. The person you should *really* be talking to is Candy Murphy."

We'd seen Candy slapping Zane at reunion, but we still didn't know why she'd done it. I didn't want Helen to have that information either if she hadn't already known, so I asked her, "So why should we consider Candy?"

"She and Zane dated in high school. Surely you both remember that," Helen said.

I had, but I hadn't thought it was all that apropos to our investigation. "That's old news," Grace said before I could. "You're not going to try to tell us that she's still upset over that."

"Not about the fact that he broke up with her," Helen said, "but that he took some photos of her that she thought had been destroyed a long time ago."

"How could you possibly know about that?" I asked her.

She blushed a little as she admitted, "I wasn't eavesdropping or anything. I just happened to be standing nearby when she confronted him about it. She slapped him hard enough to leave a mark, I can tell you that."

"How did Zane react to that?" I asked.

"He just laughed at her, which made her even angrier. Zane had a mean streak in him, and he loved it when he was in a position of power over someone else."

I saw Grace blanch a little, and I knew that I had to change the subject. "It sounds as though you know about that from first-hand experience," I said.

She nodded. "He tried to blackmail me about our night together. He even threatened to tell Henry, but since he didn't want Janet to leave him, I knew that he was bluffing."

"Let me ask you something," I said. "He treated Janet badly, so why did he even want to stay with her?" It was something that I'd been wondering about ever since I'd found out that they were together.

"You don't know? Divorcing her, or allowing her to divorce him, would have been a sign of weakness, that he'd failed at something, and that was one thing that Zane wouldn't tolerate."

"He stayed with her because of *that*?" Grace asked. It was clearly as foreign a concept to her as it was to me.

"People stay together for stranger reasons than that," Helen said, and then her phone rang. After a moment's conversation, she hung up and told us, "Sorry, but I have to go."

As she stood, I said, "Helen, you can't brush us off that easily. We need more time with you."

"That wasn't Marcy. Two students were fighting in the hallway, and I need to figure out what happened. If you'll excuse me, I have a job to do."

As we followed Helen out of her office, she said softly to me, "I'm trusting you both. Don't let me down, or none of us will be happy about it."

"Is that a threat?" I asked her just as softly.

She grinned broadly at me. "As a matter of fact, it is. I've got a good thing going here with Henry and my job, and I'd hate to see anything harm either one."

"Then maybe you should have been a little more discreet," Grace replied just as softly.

Helen's eyes narrowed, but she didn't say anything as she hurried out toward the hall.

"Wow, that was clearly a direct hit," Marcy said with more pleasure than she probably should have. "What did you just say to her?"

Grace waved it off. "I just told her to have a nice day."

"I'll bet you did," Marcy said with new respect clear in her gaze.

Once we were off school grounds, Grace said, "I should

have kept my mouth shut there at the end. I knew it as I was saying it, but I still couldn't help myself. You're not mad at me, are you?"

I shook my head and smiled. "On the contrary. Helen was a little too smug for my taste. I didn't know how to shake her up, but you did it just fine."

"I just couldn't stand how self-righteous she was being."

"Neither could I," I said.

"Do you believe what she said about Candy?" Grace asked me as we got back into the Jeep.

"It sounds spot on, doesn't it? After all, we were all young and stupid back then."

"Some of us were apparently even dumber than most," Grace said. "Why would she let him take pictures of her? How bad must they be?"

"I don't know, but there's only one way to find out," I said.

"We're going to come right out and ask her, aren't we?"

"What choice do we have? We can't exactly come out and ask Zane, can we? Candy's the only one we can talk to to see if what Helen just told us was the truth."

"I'm not looking forward to *that* conversation," Grace said.

"I'm not either," I said, "but there's no time like the present. Let's go see if we can find Candy at her gym and ask her about that slap."

"I wonder if she'll tell us the truth about it," Grace said as I started to drive away.

"It would be a refreshing change of pace, but I'm not going to hold my breath," I said.

I suddenly stopped my car, though.

"What's wrong?" Grace asked me.

I pointed to the older man pushing a trashcan on wheels away from the gymnasium. Inside it were remnants of the night's festivities, at least those that the police hadn't confiscated. An extra bonus was that it was clearly the man who'd worked during the reunion the night before. His full head of white hair made him easy enough to identify. "We need to talk to that man about what he found inside," I said as I put the transmission in Park. "There might be a clue there that Chief Martin missed."

Chapter 12

"Excuse me. Do you have a second?" I asked the older man as we approached. He was wearing a pair of crisp new coveralls with the name STEVE embroidered on them.

"What can I do for you ladies?" he asked with a smile as he stopped pushing the trashcan.

"It's about the reunion," Grace said.

Steve put a hand through his hair. "If I'd known how messy you folks were going to be, I would have asked for double time."

"I can only imagine," I said. "Have you finished cleaning up yet?"

"This is the last of it," he said as he gestured to the trashcan. "The police just cleared me to finish the job."

"You didn't happen to find the other spear holding the reunion banner, did you?" I asked him.

"Nope, they took that with them, along with almost everything else that might be considered evidence. That was okay by me. Less to clean up on my end, you know?"

I agreed, though I'd been wanting to examine the spear that had been left behind. I'd noticed them both the night before and hadn't thought anything about the decorations, but since one of them had been used to kill Zane Dunbar, their significance to me had grown quite a bit. "I saw you at the reunion," I said, though in truth I'd just noticed him on Gary's video.

"I saw you both there, too," Steve said with a grin. "I also happened to notice that neither one of you came with a date," he added as he brushed a bit of hair off his forehead. Was he actually flirting with us?

"Did you happen to notice anything out of the ordinary last night, or even today as you were cleaning up?" I asked him, deciding not to address his statement.

"Nothing worth talking about," he said. "A few geniuses thought they'd pull some pranks while they were back in school, so I've been mostly dealing with their messes."

"What kind of pranks?" Grace asked.

"You know, stupid kid stuff that grown men should know better than doing. There was plastic wrap over a few of the men's toilets, somebody stuck gum in the water fountain spouts, a few random new locks were put on some of the empty lockers in the halls, and at least ten light bulbs were unscrewed all over the place. I swear, the adults were worse than the kids ever dreamed about being. Why do you want to know all of this?"

"Let's just say that we're curious by nature," Grace answered before I could speak.

"I bet you are. Say, I'm almost finished here. Would either one of you—"

He was interrupted by his walkie-talkie. "Steve, they need you back in the gym. Somebody superglued the coach's lock shut on his door, and he can't get in."

"On my way," he replied, and then he turned to us as he pushed the trashcan to one side. "Sorry, but duty calls."

"If you find anything else interesting, call me," I said as I gave him a card from the donut shop.

"And if I want to discuss something more personal?" Steve asked.

"You'll have to take that up with my boyfriend. He's a North Carolina State Trooper."

Steve just shrugged. "It figures. Well, you can't blame a guy for trying."

He was about to turn to say something to Grace when she said quickly, "We've got to run, too."

As we got back into the Jeep, I asked, "Why did you interrupt him? I think he was about to ask you out on a date."

"Why do you think I took off like that?"

"What's wrong with him? Is it his job?" I asked her with a grin.

"I don't care what he does for a living, but the man looks like my grandfather," Grace said.

"I'm just teasing you," I said as I watched Steve in my rearview mirror. He abandoned the trash and headed back into the building. "Should we go through that trash in the can while we have a chance?"

"We can if you think it's important," she said reluctantly. "Man, I wish I had a pair of gloves, though."

"Or maybe even a Hazmat suit," I countered. "Men can be really disgusting, can't they?"

"I don't know about that. I think they're fine on their own, but when you get them back together with their high school cronies, anything can happen."

We got back out of the Jeep and approached the trashcan, but when we were just a few feet from it, another janitor came out of the building.

"Can I help you?" he asked sternly, lacking any of Steve's charm.

"We were just wondering what was left over from the reunion," Grace said quickly. "It's sentimental, you understand."

"You don't want *any* part of this. Trust me on that," the man said as he wheeled the trashcan to the dumpster and tossed it all in.

He disappeared back inside the building, and Grace and I looked in the dumpster.

After a moment, I said, "I don't know about you, but I'm not willing to go *that* far digging for clues."

"I'm sure Chief Martin and his people were more than thorough," Grace agreed. "It would just be redundant if we searched it, too."

"And if he found out that we did it, it might even hurt his feelings," I added as I caught a few whiffs of the trash.

"We wouldn't want that," Grace said, "especially since

we've both worked so hard to gain his confidence and trust."

We looked at each other for a second, and then we both burst out laughing.

"I don't care if there are hundred dollar bills at the bottom of that thing; I'm not going in," I said.

"Me, either," Grace said.

"So then, we're off to Candy's gym?" I asked.

"Look at it this way. It can't smell any worse than this."

"I hope you're right," I said as we got back into the Jeep again and drove away. As I pulled out of the parking lot, I glanced back in my rearview mirror. A face pulled quickly back into the shadows in one of the windows, and I wasn't a hundred percent positive, but I could swear that Helen Marston had been watching us. How long had she been there, and more importantly, why had she cared what we were up to? "Grace, did you just see that?"

"See what?" she asked.

I glanced over, and she was texting someone on her cellphone.

"Never mind," I said as I started driving.

"Oh, no," she said as she put her phone away. "You're not getting away with anything that easily. Talk to me, Suzanne."

"I could have sworn that I just saw Helen Marston watching us from one of the windows in the school. When she saw that I spotted her, she ducked back into the shadows. At least I *thought* it was her."

"Why would she care what we were doing?" Grace asked. "Unless she's the killer."

"Come on, I can think of more reasons than that," I countered. "Maybe she was just passing by and happened to glance out at the same time that I looked backward. It could happen."

"Sure it could, but it won't do us any good thinking like

that," Grace said.

"Even if she was watching us, that still doesn't make her a murderer," I said.

"No, but it's interesting nonetheless. Let's just file the fact away and focus on Candy. How are we going to approach her?"

"Are you interested in a gym membership?" I asked her with a sly smile.

"No, thanks. I have my own workout routines at home." After a moment's pause, she asked, "Why, do I *look* like I need to join a gym?"

"Of course not," I said. "You're fitter than I'll ever be. I just thought if you asked Candy about a membership, we might have a chance to talk to her."

"Why don't *you* join?" Grace asked.

"Everybody in town knows that I couldn't afford it," I said.

"You don't even know how much it is," Grace replied.

"I don't have to. It's still too much for me."

"Okay, I'll take the bullet for the team."

"I certainly hope not," I said, not even smiling. I hated putting Grace, or any of my friends, at risk during our investigations.

"Relax, I'm just speaking figuratively. There's just one problem, though."

"Just one?" I asked.

"If I'm there to see the gym, why are you with me?"

"Maybe you wanted a second opinion," I said.

"Sure, why not? Okay, let's do this."

We'd arrived at Candy's gym, a place she'd named The Sweet Spa and Gym. Under the name of the gym, the phrase "Where Candy Rules" was written in script.

"If this place is decorated with candy canes and lollipops, I'm leaving," Grace said. "I don't care what her first name is, candy and workouts just don't go together."

"I don't know. I've got to give her points for using what she had. Who calls their baby girl Candy, anyway? It's just *asking* for all kinds of grief for that child."

"Over the years, I've heard a lot worse," Grace said.

"Maybe so, but I still don't think that it's right."

We parked in the crowded lot and started for the front door. "You have to give her credit," Grace said. "At least the parking lot is full."

"Candy seems to be doing better for herself than I am at Donut Hearts," I replied.

"I can't imagine why," Grace said.

Once we were inside, we knew, though.

Three quarters of the people inside currently working out were men, but without a single exception, every employee was a shapely young woman wearing a red leotard and white hose.

Then it hit me; they were all dressed like candy canes.

"Do you like our look?" Candy asked as she approached us. To be fair, she wore the same outfit as her employees, and she made it look good. "I just love themes, don't you?"

"Do you have any women who are members?" I asked.

"Quite a few, actually," Candy said, "though we do seem to skew heavily toward men. What can I do for you?"

"Actually, I'm thinking about joining up," Grace said.

Candy's smile was practiced, but it was still kind of infectious. "Excellent. What about you, Suzanne? Will you be joining us as well?"

"I'm just here for moral support at the moment," I said.

"Trust me, after you see what we have to offer, you'll want to sign up yourself. Are you both ready for the tour of our facilities?"

"We are," Grace said.

It was a typical gym, despite the brightly-painted murals of candy and the lovely staff members. Weights were in one section, treadmills and elliptical machines had their own spot, and there was a dedicated area filled with machines that I couldn't even guess about their uses. In spite of why we were really there, I couldn't help but ask, "I see the gym, but where's the spa part?"

"That's going to be phase two," she said as she described special massage areas, contemplation rooms, and a yoga studio.

"That's an ambitious dream," Grace said.

Candy smiled, this one more genuine than the one that she'd greeted us with. "As far as I'm concerned, if you don't dream, then you might as well be dead," she said.

"Speaking of dead, it's terrible about what happened to Zane, isn't it?" Grace asked.

Candy's smile vanished. "Is that why you're here? I thought you wanted to see my gym?"

"Why can't it be both?" Grace asked.

"Because I know you two better than you might think. Why are you really here?"

It was time to drop the ruse. "A reliable source told us about your relationship with Zane."

Candy laughed. "Is that all you've got? *Everybody* knows that Zane and I dated in high school. It's not exactly news, is it?"

"Candy, we heard about the pictures he took of you," I said softly. "I can't imagine a lot of folks know about that."

She looked as though she'd been shot in the chest. Candy physically flinched as her smile vanished and her face went white.

"Are you okay?" I asked as I put out a hand to steady her.

"I'm fine," she said, taking a deep breath and shaking her head slightly. "No one was supposed to know about those. Have you seen them?"

"No," I said before Grace could imply that we had. I wasn't certain that was what she was going to do, but I couldn't rule it out, either. "How bad are they?"

"By today's standards, they're pretty tame stuff," she said.

"But they still aren't something you want getting out, are they?" Grace asked.

"Not on your life. I'm building something here," she said as she gestured around the large expanse with her hands. "Any scandal right now could ruin everything."

"Come on. It can't be that bad, not if the pictures are as mild as you say they are," I said.

"My main investor is pretty conservative," Candy said. "Any hint of this kind of scandal could make him pull the plug on my entire operation."

"Then it must have been pretty important to keep Zane from showing the pictures around."

Candy nodded, and then she caught herself. "Hang on a second. I didn't kill him."

"You certainly had motive, means, and plenty of opportunity," I said.

"So did several other people at that reunion," she countered quickly. "Zane had a *pile* of enemies. Besides, why would I kill him? He told me that if anything happened to him, the pictures would get out. My only prayer was that he stayed healthy. I don't know what's going to happen to me now. I've been dreading the knock on my door ever since I heard that he was murdered."

Candy made a good point, but that depended on her acting logically. If she felt threatened, common sense might have gone out the window, and she could have killed him out of sheer fear. The cause of death certainly reflected that. I couldn't imagine killing someone, but if I were ever to consider it, it certainly wouldn't be using a spear to stab them in the chest. That would take an emotional outburst at a level that I hoped I never hit myself. "If you didn't do it, then you have nothing to worry about," Grace said.

Candy sighed heavily. "I just wish that were really

true."

A young woman dressed in the company uniform approached. She also wore a bright pink button that said her name was Bubblegum. I frankly doubted that was true. "Candy, I'm sorry to bother you, but we've got a problem with Mr. Jefferson again."

"What's he done this time?" Candy asked.

"He keeps making comments about my outfit," she said with a frown.

"Don't worry about it. I'll talk to him," Candy said.

"He's so old and creepy. He must be over thirty," she said as she wrinkled her nose.

"Go take over at the front desk," Candy said, and then she turned to us. "I'm sorry, but I have to handle this."

"Is he *really* creepy, or is she just put off by his age? Thirty? Seriously?"

Candy shook her head. "She tends to over-exaggerate, but she's a good worker, and he's a good client, so I need to go deal with this. Sorry."

"It's fine," I said as Grace and I made our way out of the gym.

Once we were outside, Grace asked me, "Do you believe her?"

"I want to," I said. "It certainly all has its own internal logic."

"Then again, she's pretty smooth. We may have both just been played by someone who is better at this than we are."

"To be fair, it sounds as though she's had a lot more practice than we have," I said.

"So what comes next?" Grace asked me as we got back into the Jeep.

I glanced at my watch and saw that it was nearly six. "If it's okay with you, I want to check in with Momma."

"What's going on?" Grace asked.

"Nothing, but if she's made a big meal, I'm going to feel bad about it."

"Why's that?"

"Grace, we ate a big lunch, and then we both had way too much pasta at Napoli's. Do you honestly believe that you could eat another meal at this point?"

"It depends on what she's serving," Grace said with a grin. "Your mother is a wonderful cook."

"You're bluffing," I said.

"Try me."

I called Momma, who picked up on the first ring. "I was just about to call you, Suzanne."

"What's up, Momma? Did you cook tonight?"

A hint of guilt crept into her voice. "Phillip has asked me to dinner. You know we haven't had much time together lately, and with this murder on his desk now, we might not be able to do it again in ages. Do you mind fending for yourself tonight?"

"I'll be fine. Grace and I may do something together."

"That would be lovely. Don't wait up," she said happily, and I could hear a buoyancy in her voice that I loved. I'd been skeptical about her dating our chief of police at first, but seeing how happy he made my mother had gone a long way to easing my concerns. He lightened her somehow, and I would never begrudge her that, particularly because Jake had done the same thing for me.

"Have fun," I said.

"Oh, of that you can be sure."

After I hung up, I turned to Grace and said, "It looks as though we're on our own tonight. Are you going to be able to survive not having a fourth meal today?"

"I'll find a way to manage," she said with a smile. "So what are these two wild and crazy girls going to do tonight? Should we go out on the town and live it up?"

"I was thinking about calling in a pizza later and watching a video," I said.

"Oh, a movie sounds like fun," Grace said.

"That's not the video I was talking about. I want

another look at Gary's footage from last night."

"Then it's a good thing I kept a copy on my computer," she said.

"Do you mind if we stay in tonight?" I asked her.

"As a matter of fact, that sounds great. We can even do it at my house, since your mother isn't going to be home."

"Wonderful," I said as I started driving to her place. We seemed to be at my house a great deal of the time, so it would be nice hanging out with Grace in her home.

Hopefully, tonight we'd have a good meal, a few laughs, and maybe even be able to find another clue or two lurking in the video recording of what had happened at the reunion last night.

Chapter 13

My phone rang just as we got to Grace's house.

"Hi, Emma," I said as I pulled in and shut off the engine. "What's up?"

"Hey, Suzanne. Is this a good time to talk?"

"Sure. Hang on for one second, okay?" I asked, and then I held my hand over the phone and told Grace, "It's Emma. I'll be right in."

"Is anything wrong?" Grace asked.

I shrugged. "I don't think so," I said, and then I asked Emma, "Is anything wrong?"

"No, not on my end."

"Good," I said. "One more second." I told Grace, "No, it's good. I'll see you inside."

"I'll go ahead and call the pizza in," Grace said.

"Just get a medium. I'm still full from the 'snack' we had at Napoli's."

"You say that now, but we both know how long delivery takes. I'm going ahead and getting a large anyway."

"Suit yourself," I said. "I'm just warning you that I'm not going to eat a ton of it."

"I won't hold you to that when it gets here," she said with a grin and headed inside.

"Sorry about that," I said as I turned my attention back to Emma. "Go ahead."

"Did I catch you at a bad time? This can wait."

"No, you've got my complete and undivided attention," I said. "How did things go today?"

"It was all good," Emma said. "With Mom there, it was even kind of fun. That's why I'm calling. We're willing to do it again tomorrow if you need more time to investigate."

I considered it for a moment, but I knew that I couldn't

abandon Donut Hearts two days in a row. Besides, there was another pressing reason for me to show up at the donut shop the next day. "Thanks, but I'm coming in. Tomorrow's my book club, and I wouldn't miss that for the world. You don't have to show up, though, if you don't want to."

"I'm always happy to work," she said.

"I know that, but I put you on the spot today, and you came through with flying colors. If you don't want to take the day off completely, how about sleeping in instead?"

"Now *that* sounds like a deal. How about if I come by an hour later than normal?"

I might regret it, but I decided to match the time that I'd been gone. "We can do better than that. Come in a few minutes before six, and I should be fine on my own until then."

"Are you sure?" she asked me.

"At this second, yes, but I wouldn't take too long considering the offer," I said.

She must have heard the grin in my voice. "Sold. See you tomorrow around six. Thanks, Suzanne."

"Thank you, and thank your mother for me, too."

"She *loves* helping out," Emma said.

"I appreciate that. Let her know that I'll send a little something her way this week for lending a hand."

"She won't say no to that. She's saving up to take a trip to Hawaii."

That was surprising to hear, since Ray Blake was as fanatical about his newspaper as I was about my donut shop. "Did your father actually agree to go with her?"

Emma laughed. "Are you kidding? He's not about to leave his little baby. Mom's going with her best friend from high school. She's going to have a blast."

"It sounds like fun. Thanks for calling. I'll see you in the morning, Emma."

"But not too early," she said, laughing again. She

seemed more excited about coming in late than she had at the prospect of taking the entire day off.

I came in to find Grace watching the video again. "I thought you were going to order a pizza," I said as I sat down beside her on the sofa.

"I already did," she said. "What did Emma want?"

"She asked me if I wanted to take tomorrow off so we could sleuth again."

"And what did you say to that?" Grace asked me after a slight hesitation.

"I told her that I was going to work a full shift at the donut shop tomorrow. Is that okay with you?"

"Honestly, I'm kind of relieved. I have some work that I need to do in the morning, too, but I was going to blow it off if you wanted to dig into Zane's murder more. I can't even seem to keep from working when I'm on vacation."

I laughed at her. "Aren't we a pair of workaholics?" I asked

"You more than me. I've just got quarterly reports due, and not enough time to do them. My boss lets me run my own show here, but she's a maniac when it comes to those reports."

"Good. I'm glad that's settled," I said as I gestured to the screen. "Did you find anything new so far?"

"Not yet," she said. "We were pretty thorough the first time around."

As I settled in, I nodded. "I understand that it's a long shot, but I don't know what else we can do at this point. We can't just keep asking people questions until someone gives us a lead."

"Why not? It's worked for us in the past."

"Occasionally, but not always," I said. "There's got to be something we're missing, some clue that we've overlooked."

"What makes you say that?" Grace asked as she hit the

Pause key.

"I don't know," I replied. "Something in my gut tells me that there are a few pieces that I'm not connecting yet. Don't worry, I'll figure it out eventually. Maybe this video will jog my memory."

"If nothing else, we get to see how far downhill our classmates have gone again," Grace said with a grin.

"Including us," I added.

"I was about to say *excluding* us," she said as she hit Play again.

We watched the entire thing without stopping it once. Gary's documentary about the reunion was still the same, though I did notice a few things I'd missed before. As the camera panned by the bathrooms, I thought about the pranks the men had perpetrated, from the clear plastic wrap to the new locks to the glue in the coach's door. Why did so many men seem to take so much longer to grow up than we did? Maybe that wasn't fair, though. I couldn't imagine Jake *ever* doing anything like my former classmates had done, and I doubted that our mayor or our chief of police had ever participated in that kind of behavior. Clearly, the men who had acted so immaturely at the reunion were still boys inside.

The pizza came as we were watching the video, so we ate companionably as we watched. "This is really good," I said as I finished my second slice. "I'm glad you got a large after all."

"Hey, I've seen us both eat before," Grace said happily. "It's just too bad the entertainment isn't any better. Have you seen *anything* to add to our fact base so far?"

"No, but I'm still hopeful," I said as I grabbed another piece without even debating it.

After the video was finished, Grace turned it off and turned to me. "Well, that was a complete waste of time, wasn't it?"

"I don't know. The pizza was good," I answered.

"I'm talking about our search for clues," she replied.

"I knew what you meant. It was a long shot, but I'm still glad that we tried. It's not like we don't have enough viable suspects as things stand now."

"Should we go over them again?" Grace asked as she pulled out a new whiteboard and marker.

"Did you get that just for our detective work?" I asked.

"Actually, I'm supposed to be using it to track the sales quotas for my underlings," she said, "but why not use it for both?" Grace took the marker and wrote the names of our suspects down one side of the board: TOM HANCOCK, BILLY BRISCOE, JANET DUNBAR, HENRY DAVIDSON, HELEN MARSTON, and CANDY MURPHY. "Did I miss anybody?"

"Not unless there's a long shot that we haven't even considered yet," I said. As I studied the board, I added, "Wow, that's quite the list, isn't it?"

"Zane had a way of polarizing people, didn't he?" Grace asked as she added another column, this one headed MOTIVE.

"Here it gets a little trickier," she said as she paused at the first name. "Tom either owed Zane money he couldn't or didn't want to pay back, or he was up to something else," she said as she made a dollar sign beside Tom's name.

"Put a heart beside Janet's name," I said. "Most women kill their husbands out of affairs of the heart."

"Maybe, but she might have wanted that insurance money more than a husband," Grace replied as she added another dollar sign beside the heart.

"What kind of symbol are you going to use for Henry?" I asked.

"It has to be a heart, since his motive was defending Helen," she said as she drew it. "Helen gets one, too."

"Maybe we're being a little too simplistic here," I said as I studied the symbols we'd used so far.

"This is just our shorthand," Grace said. "We know what we mean."

"Okay. What about Candy?"

Grace drew a little ghost.

"Seriously? Why a ghost?"

"Because she was afraid of being exposed, and I mean that literally," Grace said. "Most people are afraid of ghosts, right?" she asked me with a smile.

"I can't argue with that," I said. "My question is, how do we go about eliminating some of those names?"

"That's the real question here, isn't it?"

"Do you have any ideas?" I asked her.

"Not off the top of my head, but I'll think better after a good night's sleep."

As if on cue, I yawned. "Me, too."

"Let's pack it in, Suzanne. It's been a big day, and we're both working tomorrow."

"But we're still working on the case tomorrow afternoon, right?" I asked her.

"We are," she said. "What time is good for you to get started?"

"I'll be free around eleven if you can be," I said as she walked me out to my Jeep.

"Make it noon and you've got a deal," Grace said.

"Noon it is. That will give me time to come home, take a shower, and change."

"Then we can have lunch and then start digging again after that," Grace answered.

"I'll see you tomorrow, then. Sleep tight."

"You, too."

To my surprise, Momma was home when I pulled into the driveway, and lights were on inside the house. Had something happened to end her date prematurely?

"Hey," I said as I walked into the house. "What are you doing here? Is everything all right?"

"Everything is just fine," Momma said as she looked up from her e-reader. She was on the couch sitting in front of a blazing fire, and yet she still had a blanket tucked around her. Momma enjoyed being toasty a great deal more than I did, and if I couldn't crack my window on the second floor every now and then to let in a little cool air, I would have had a tough time sleeping at night.

"I thought you had a date tonight," I said as I took a seat across from her.

"Phillip was called back to the office unexpectedly," she said.

Had there been a break in the case? I wanted so much to ask her, but I'd made it a rule not to quiz my mother about what her boyfriend was doing, especially when it involved a murder we were both investigating. "I'm sorry. Did you at least get a chance to eat?"

"I did, and thank you."

"For what?"

"For not asking me anything else about it," she said as she put her reader aside.

"You're welcome," I said. "How's your book?"

"As a matter of fact, I'm reading the same one you and your book club are discussing tomorrow," she said. "It sounded interesting when you told me about it. Right now I'm on page ninety-three. Have you finished it yet?"

"I read it a few nights ago," I said. "What do you think so far?"

"It's good, but I want to wait to see how it ends before I pass final judgment on it," she said. "I believe I know who did it, and how it was done."

"I'll bet you an apple pie that you don't," I said with a grin.

Momma frowned. "Is that a spoiler, Suzanne?"

"No, ma'am. I wouldn't do that to you."

"Then let's not talk about it anymore," she said. "How is your investigation going?"

"Well, right now we have a ton of suspects, and instead of eliminating any, we keep adding more. Who knew that a high school reunion could bring out so much of the bad in people?"

"Why are you surprised?" she asked. "When you mix buried hard feelings with alcohol, it's doubtful that no one's going to get hurt."

"I understand a black eye or two, but murder?"

"Sometimes slights from the past become magnified over time to the point where they consume the person who felt wronged."

I thought about that for a moment, and then I asked, "So then you think it's more likely that Zane's murder was because of something in his past rather than his present?"

"I'm not saying that," Momma explained. "All I'm saying is that it was a volatile situation. Have you seen the widow yet?"

"I spoke with her today," I said.

"She must be grief-stricken," Momma said.

"You'd think so, wouldn't you?"

"From your tone, I'm guessing that she's not."

"Momma, she's already called the insurance company, and the man hasn't been dead for even a day yet. How does someone do that?"

She shook her head slowly. "Suzanne, she might not even realize emotionally that he's gone yet. Don't judge her too harshly today. We have no idea what went on between them in their marriage. She must be feeling a hundred different emotions right now."

In a soft voice, I asked her, "Is that how it was when Dad died?"

She sighed long and loud, and then Momma said, "All I felt then was grief. I still miss your father every day. That hasn't changed since the day he died, and no matter what happens in my future, I suspect that it never will."

"I'm so sorry," I said as I reached over and patted her hand.

"Don't be," Momma said with a gentle smile. "I have a world of memories of our time together, and despite a few rocky patches, I wouldn't have traded any of it for the world." She wiped away a tear from her cheek, and then she added, "It's getting late. Hadn't you better be off to bed?"

I glanced at the clock and saw that she was right. Most people would be hours away from sleep, but then again, they didn't have to keep my hours, either. "You're right. Good night."

"Good night," she said.

I glanced down at her as I went up the stairs, and she'd already opened her e-reader again. I just hoped that she wasn't as disappointed with the ending of that book as I'd been. I couldn't wait to discuss it with my friends the next day. My book club had come into Donut Hearts one day looking for a place to hold their meetings, and they'd gladly welcomed me to join them. It was one of the regular things in my life that I counted on and looked forward to every month, and I was glad they'd randomly chosen my shop that day.

It was odd the next morning being at the donut shop without Emma, even though I ran the place one day a week without her. Maybe it was because I'd had time to get used to it then. This was different. I could swear I heard noises coming from the front of the shop as I worked in the kitchen, but every time I walked out there, I was all alone. By the time my break came as the yeast donut dough rose, I was having second thoughts about going outside, even though it was part of my routine. The fresh air always did me good, but the dark seemed a little more ominous today that it normally did.

"Stop being such a sissy and go outside," I said aloud to myself.

I took a deep breath, and then I walked out of the shop into the brisk morning air. Just in case, though, I didn't go far, and I left the door unlocked behind me in case I had to dash back inside.

When my cellphone rang, I nearly jumped out of my

skin.

It was Jake!

"Hey there," I said, trying to keep the edge of unease I'd been feeling out of my voice.

"Is this a bad time?" he asked. It was clear how exhausted he was by the strain in his voice.

"It's perfect. I'm on my break," I said. "How are you doing?"

"I'm worn out," he said.

"How's the case going?"

"Frustrating. I thought I had him, but it turned out to be a bad tip. The worst part is that he struck again four hours ago." The anger and disappointment in his voice were both easy to read.

"Don't give up hope, Jake. You'll get him," I said.

"It sure doesn't feel like it," he said. "How's your case going?"

"About like normal. I have more suspects than I know what to do with, and it's aggravating."

"At least you *have* suspects," Jake said. "Tell me about what you've been doing."

"Are you sure you want to hear about Zane's murder? You must be sick of killing by now."

"Who knows? Maybe you'll say something that will spark an idea in me. Besides, it's relaxing to hear you talk."

"I'm not sure if that's a compliment or not," I said with a grin.

"Trust me, it is. Talk to me, Suzanne."

I went over everything Grace and I had discussed the night before, and by the time I was finished, I asked, "So do you have any ideas for me?"

"It sounds as though you're on the right track," he said. "You have to keep pressing your suspects. Sooner or later, somebody's going to crack."

"I don't have that luxury," I said. "After all, nobody *has* to talk to me."

"That's true," he said. "Still, I have faith in you."

"Aren't we a pair?" I asked.

"I like to think so," he said.

Just then, the timer beside me went off, indicating that my break was over. I planned to ignore it, but Jake must have heard it. "What was that?"

"My timer," I said. "It's okay, though."

"It certainly is not," Jake said. "You've got donuts to make, and I need a few hours of sleep before I get up and start all over again."

"Thanks for calling," I said.

"Would it surprise you to know that talking to you has been the highlight of an otherwise dreadful day, Suzanne?"

"I would hope so," I said happily. "Call any time."

"I might. Good night, my love."

"Good morning," I said, and I knew that he had to hear me smiling as I said it.

I hung up, took a deep breath of air, and suddenly realized that the fear and trepidation I'd been feeling before about being alone was gone. Just hearing Jake's voice had been all the tonic that I needed. I was ready to take on the world.

I still locked the donut shop door behind me after I walked in, though.

After all, there was no reason to be foolish about it. No matter how good I felt at the moment, there was still a murderer loose on the streets of April Springs, and I was going to keep watching my back until someone brought them to justice.

Chapter 14

"Good morning," I said as Emma walked in a few minutes before six. "Tell me, what was it like sleeping in?"

She yawned a little as she stretched. "It was awesome," she said. "Did you miss me?"

"As a matter of fact, I did. I tried to do a few dishes, but I'm afraid there's quite a stack in there waiting for you."

"I'm happy to do them. You don't think we could make this a full-time thing, could you? I could see the advantages of working five hours a day six days a week."

"That sounds good to me," I said with a smile. Before she could respond, I added, "Of course, I'll only be able to pay you for the hours that you're actually here working."

Emma laughed at my suggestion. "Never mind. I like the old system just fine. It was really nice, though. You should let my mother and me make the donuts one day a week without you. If you feel the need, you could come in at six like I am today. I'm telling you, Suzanne, once you try it, you'll never be able to go back."

"That's what I'm afraid of," I said as I brought the last tray of donuts out and slid them into the display case. "I know myself too well. I'll get spoiled, and then I won't want to come in on time ever again. Before you know it, we're both going to be out looking for a job. I appreciate the offer, but for right now, let's just stick with what works."

"That's fine by me," she said. "Have you picked up a copy of the newspaper yet?"

"No, I've been kind of busy getting ready to open," I said with a smile. "Is there something new and noteworthy that I've missed?"

"Dad's got a full page article on Zane's murder. It's got something interesting stuff in it." She brought a paper out from the folds of her heavy jacket and presented it to me. "Extra, extra, read all about it."

"Thanks," I said.

"I'll be in back if you need me," Emma said.

She left me alone up front, and since we didn't have any customers clamoring to get in, after I unlocked the door and flipped the sign to show that we were open, I took out the newspaper to see what Ray Blake had gotten wrong this time.

As I suspected, it was full of supposition, innuendo, and conjecture. There wasn't anything actionable that I could see, but he sure didn't take it easy on the murder victim. I doubted that Janet would be able to sue him for libel, but that didn't mean that Ray had pulled any punches. There was enough shading in the article to imply that Zane had deserved exactly what he'd gotten. I wasn't even all that surprised. Ray had a reputation for not letting facts stand in the way of a good story, and he hadn't done anything to negate that impression in his paper. What's more, Ray had focused more on the mischiefs some of the former students had performed, making them somehow related to Zane's death, though I didn't see how that was possible. Who cared that pranks had been set up in the bathrooms on the most juvenile level, or that several new locks were found on previously empty lockers, or that the coach's door had been glued shut? All in all, it wasn't worth the time that it had taken to read it.

"I'd like three dozen of your prettiest donuts to go," a young woman said a little after seven.

"You don't even care about how they taste?" I asked. It was an odd enough request to catch my attention, and I wanted to know her motivation for her order.

"I'm sure they're all delicious, but we're celebrating over at the high school," she said.

"What's the happy occasion?" I asked as I started adding sprinkled donuts, colorful cake donuts, and brightly iced yeast donuts to the boxes.

"One of our teachers just married our guidance counselor," she said.

I nearly dropped the full box of donuts in my hand. "Henry Davidson and Helen Marston got *married*? When did this happen?"

"Oh, do you know them? It was the night before last," she said. "They didn't want to say anything right away, given the bad timing and everything."

"What timing is that?" I asked as I recovered enough to start stocking another box.

"They *had* been planning on having a formal wedding sometime next month, but right after they left the reunion, they decided to drive straight to the beach to elope. Once they got there, they woke up a justice of the peace and got married at two in the morning. It's really romantic, isn't it?"

"It sure is," I said as I started doing the math in my head. We were a good five hours from the beach, and that matched up if they left at nine. Unfortunately, that gave them a tight alibi, because they couldn't have made it back before seven, well after I'd found Zane's body. "I would have thought they would have said something before this, though."

"They told their family, but no one else knew. It's all so exciting."

I finished packing the third box of donuts and slid them across the counter to her. After I quoted her the price, she paid gladly with a fifty-dollar bill, and as I gave her the change, she was beaming with delight. "Tell them that Suzanne from Donut Hearts said congratulations," I said.

"I will," she said. "You should see the teacher's

lounge. Becky, Tonya, and I have been decorating it since five this morning. Everything's just perfect."

"It sounds lovely," I said as she left the shop.

I probably should have given her the donuts free of charge, since she'd just unwittingly eliminated two of my strongest suspects. There were a lot of reasons to believe that either Henry or Helen could have done it, but none of that mattered now. I'd tell the police chief so he could confirm their story, but I had a hunch that it was true. That meant striking their names off our list of suspects. That still left Tom, Janet, Billy, and Candy, but at least it had cleared up a little room for us. Having six suspects was a bit overwhelming, while four was a little more manageable. Grace and I had to narrow the list of names down even further if we were hoping to solve Zane's murder before the rumors started flying about Grace as a possible suspect. So far, no one had pointed any fingers at her, but that might have had more to do with the friendship that Grace and I shared than the town's belief that she was innocent of murder. Either way, we were in a rush to track down the killer, and as soon as I closed the donut shop for the day, we'd renew our hunt.

"Suzanne, do you have a second?" I was shocked to see Tom Hancock in my donut shop asking me for *my* time.

"Sure, Tom. Would you like a donut?"

"Sorry, but I don't have time for that," Tom said as he waved a hand in the air. He looked around the shop at the dozen folks enjoying their treats and added, "Is there someplace a little more private we can talk?"

He was a suspect high on my list, so when I heard him say "private," red flags appeared. "How private are we talking about?"

"I'm not trying to get you alone in a dark room," he snapped, and then, in a nicer voice, he added, "I just don't want anyone listening in on our conversation.

Please?"

"Okay," I said. "Give me one minute."

"Thanks. I appreciate that. I'll be outside waiting for you," he said.

I went in the back and found Emma washing dishes. "Emma?" I shouted, since she never washed them without her music blasted high.

"Hey, take it easy, Suzanne. You don't have to shout," Emma said.

"What happened to your music?"

"Can you believe it? I forgot it at home," she admitted. "I wasn't used to sleeping in, so I got up later than I should have, and then I was rushing around to make it here in time. Funny, isn't it?"

"Hilarious. Listen, I need you to cover the front."

"That's fair," she said as she pulled her hands out of the soapy water. "Will you be back in time to close, or should I take care of it myself?"

"I'll only be gone five minutes," I said. "Listen, if my book club shows up, tell them that I'll be right back, but that they can go ahead and get started without me if they want to."

"I can do that," she said as she rinsed her hands and dried them off.

Emma followed me out front, and I left her at the counter while I went off in search of Tom.

He was standing edgily across the street, and he waved to me to join him the moment he saw me.

When I reached him, I asked, "What's up?"

"Suzanne, I'm in some serious trouble," he said, and one look at the expression on his face told me that he was dead serious. "Can we walk around the park while we talk? I feel kind of exposed just standing here."

"That's fine," I said, knowing that I'd only go so far into the trees with this man before I'd stop. I'd fought killers there before who'd wanted to hurt me, and I knew how dangerous being alone with someone could be.

"What can I do?"

"For starters, you can help me figure out what to do," he said.

"I'll try, but I'm going to need a little more than that."

Tom ran a hand through his hair. "Honestly, I don't even know where to start."

"I've always found that if all else fails, the beginning is as good a place as any."

He shook his head. "Neither one of us has that much time. First things first. I didn't kill Zane."

"Okay," I said, keeping my voice neutral.

"You don't believe me, do you?" he asked.

"I'm willing to accept it for now," I said.

He was angry now. "Are you serious?"

"Hey, I'm not going to lie to you. You either want my help or you don't."

"I want it."

"Then tell me what's got you so spooked," I suggested.

"I'm the one who stole the spear from the gym the night Zane was murdered."

"You what!"

"Keep your voice down, would you?" Tom asked. "I don't want the world to know how stupid I was."

"Sorry," I said, lowering my voice to a more normal tone. "Why did you take it?"

"I wanted a souvenir, if you can believe that. As the reunion broke up, I grabbed one of the spears and took it outside. I admit that I was more than a little drunk when I took it."

"You would have had to be, wouldn't you?" I asked.

"Are you judging me, Suzanne?"

"Tom, this would go a lot faster if you'd just tell me what you did with the spear after you left the gym."

He nodded. "Fine. The second I got it outside, I realized how stupid I'd look carrying it to my car, so I dumped it."

"Where exactly did you leave it?"

"In the dumpster outside of the gymnasium," he said. "I've been trying to figure out what to do since I found out how Zane was murdered, but I can't come up with any scenario that doesn't end with me being tried for murder. My fingerprints were all over that thing, and as soon as the police figure it out, I'm dead."

"Not necessarily," I said. "Maybe the killer smudged them when he grabbed it."

"Don't you get it? Whoever did it *had* to have seen me dump it. I'm pretty sure they'd be smart enough not to wipe my prints off. It would kind of defeat the purpose, wouldn't it?"

I thought about it, and then I said, "You still might be okay for now. If your prints aren't in the system, they won't know it's you right away."

He looked instantly miserable. "I was in the ROTC in college. I'm in the system."

"Then why hasn't the chief come looking for you yet?"

Tom shrugged. "For all I know, he has. I haven't been home since the murder. I've been staying on a friend's couch."

"Tom, if you're innocent, you've got to tell Chief Martin what happened."

He looked at me as though I'd lost my mind. "*That's* your suggestion? I'll be in jail before lunch if I do anything that stupid."

"What do you want from me?" I asked.

"I don't know," he said angrily. "Everybody talks about how you're this great detective. You've got to do *something*."

"There's only one thing I can tell you at this point. Call Chief Martin."

"You're no help at all!"

"I'm sorry, but it's the only thing that might help."

He looked around, and that's when he must have realized how close we were to Grace's house. "Forget I even asked. I'll get help from someone else."

As he started toward Grace's place, I said loudly, "Leave her alone, Tom. She can't help you, either."

"We'll just see about that," he said, walking faster.

I couldn't stop him, but there was one thing that I could do.

I pulled my cellphone out of my pocket and called her. I had to warn Grace that trouble was on its way.

She didn't pick up.

Of course not. That would have been too easy.

I couldn't go back for my Jeep; I didn't have time.

Instead, I started running, hoping to head him off before he got there.

I stopped before I reached him, though.

Grace must not have seen either one of us in the park as she drove past us on her way out of town.

I called again, and this time she picked up.

"Grace," I rasped as I tried to catch my breath.

"If this is someone's attempt to get a cheap thrill, you're wasting your time. Heavy breathing on a phone is for twelve-year-olds."

"Grace, it's Suzanne," I said as I turned and hurried back to the donut shop. At least I'd caught my breath.

"Suzanne, what are you doing, trying to prank me?"

"No, this is serious. Stay away from your house."

"Now you sound like one of those teen horror movies," Grace said.

"I mean it. Tom Hancock is looking for you."

"Why exactly am I avoiding him?" she asked.

"He's the one who stole the spear from the gym, but he claims he didn't use it to kill Zane," I replied, and then I gave her the full story he had just shared with me.

"What does he want from me?" Grace asked, all of the humor now gone from her voice.

"I couldn't help him, so he decided that only you could."

"If there's nothing that *you* can do for him, I'm certainly at a loss. He should probably call the police chief. That's what I would tell him. Running away isn't going to solve anything."

"I told him that, but it's not going to be that easy."

"What are you going to do?" Grace asked me.

"What can I do? I'm calling Chief Martin."

She paused for a few moments, and then she asked, "You really don't have any choice, do you?"

"I don't think so, either. If there's a chance that the police chief *doesn't* know about this already, he has every right to know as soon as possible."

"Hang up and call him, then."

"You aren't going back home anytime soon, are you?" I asked her.

"No, I couldn't get any work done there, so I'm going to the library."

"That's a good idea. He'll never look for you there," I said.

"Hey, is that a crack, Suzanne? I might not read as much as you or your mother, but I like a good book as much as the next gal, particularly if it's a mystery."

"I didn't mean anything by it, I promise," I said. "I just think that you should be safe there."

"Okay then. I'll see you at noon. You know what? Make it eleven. I'm going to need a break from paperwork by then anyway."

"See you then," I said, and then I dialed Chief Martin's number before I could change my mind. I might just be giving a murderer a reason to come after me, but I couldn't let that stop me.

This was too important.

Chapter 15

"Thanks, but I already know about Tom Hancock's prints on the spear," the chief said. "Do you happen to know where he is right now?"

"The last time I saw him, he was on foot making his way to Grace's place. That was about five minutes ago, so he still should be close by."

"And you didn't warn her?" he barked at me.

"She was already gone," I said.

"I've been looking for Tom Hancock all day. Thanks for calling, Suzanne," the chief said.

I was about to tell him that Tom had proclaimed his innocence to me, but I would have been talking to a dead phone.

He'd already hung up on me.

Well, I'd done my civic duty. Now it was up to him. After all, the police had resources that I could only dream about, and enough manpower to conduct their own manhunt.

All I could do was ask around and hope that someone I spoke to knew something that might help me solve the crime.

It wasn't exactly a fair fight between the two of us.

I walked back into the donut shop to find Hazel, Jennifer, and Elizabeth already there, sipping on their coffees. My book club was occupying our best sofa and chairs, but their books weren't out yet.

"I'm sorry I'm late," I said. "You could have gotten started without me."

Jennifer, a bright redhead who was the leader of our little group, smiled at me. "We weren't about to do that. What fun would that be?"

"Can I get you all something to snack on?" I asked. "I made some wonderful apple fritters this morning with fresh apples."

"How many calories does each one have?" Hazel asked. The woman was always on a diet, and I felt a bit devilish whenever we met, since I had so many tasty temptations in my shop.

"I don't have a clue," I admitted.

Elizabeth, the member of our group who prided herself on corresponding with several authors, said, "Hazel, they're practically health food."

"What makes you say that?" Hazel asked her.

"You heard the woman. They have *apples* in them. I'll take one, Suzanne."

"How about you two?" I asked.

"Count me in," Jennifer said.

Hazel was still on the fence as she asked, "Are you having one, Suzanne?"

My jeans were getting a little tighter every day, but those fritters looked delicious, and I wasn't immune to my own wares. "I will if you do. We could always split one," I suggested.

"No, if you're willing to risk it, then so am I," she said. "I'll take a whole one."

I wasn't quite sure how to take that, but I smiled anyway. "Coming right up."

Emma had been listening to us chat, so she plated four fritters for us. "Take your time, Suzanne. It's kind of nice being up here where all of the action is."

I smiled at her. "Thanks. Emma, are you coming out of your shell?" She hadn't always been a fan of waiting on folks at the front counter.

"Maybe a little bit," she said. "Who knows? In a few years, you might be able to actually take a week off and have a real vacation."

"I live to dream," I said with a smile as I grabbed the plates.

After I passed them out to my group, I said, "Thanks again for waiting."

"We were happy to do it," Jennifer said. "Now, let's talk about *Murder for the Birds*. How did you all like it?"

"I have to admit that I wasn't a fan of the idea of reading a bird lovers mystery, but it was mostly good," Hazel said as she nibbled around the edges of her fritter as though it was the only thing she was going to be eating that day. I sincerely hoped that wasn't true.

"The character development was good, but the murder method was a little too outlandish for my taste," I said, and then I took a hearty bite of my fritter. There was an explosion of apple, cinnamon, and rich dense bread in my mouth. Every component complemented the whole, and I marveled sometimes at just how good I was in the kitchen. I decided to keep that last observation to myself.

"Every *one* of her plots are outlandish," Elizabeth said. "That's her niche."

"What, crazy ways to kill people?" Jennifer asked.

"I didn't think that it was *that* outlandish," Elizabeth said, always trying to take up for the authors of the books that we discussed.

I couldn't help it. "Who could even come up with a murder committed that way?" I asked. "I mean, seriously. She had the killer put birdseed on a steel plate that led to the trigger of a gun aimed at the victim's chair. When that bird pecked at the seed and killed Mary Lou, I nearly dropped the book from laughing so hard."

"It *could* have happened that way," Elizabeth said a little weakly. "Mary Lou loved watching the birds eat as she sat in her special chair. The whole town knew it, including the killer. It wouldn't have been hard to rig the entire thing up that way."

"I don't know," I said. "Give me a good old-fashioned steel pipe any day."

"I like a *blend* of murder weapons, myself," Hazel said.

"Other than that, how did you like the book?" Jennifer asked.

"She can write a great cozy. I'll give her that much," I said.

Elizabeth took that as a triumph. "That's all that I'm saying."

I took another bite of my fritter and smiled, not from the delightful treat, but from being in the presence of these nice, smart women who had adopted me into their group. That book club was something that I looked forward to every month, and the time always passed by far too quickly for my taste, even when I was in the middle of a real-life murder investigation of my own.

After the ladies in my group were gone, I took the front back over from Emma. Before she went to the back to finish the dishes, she asked, "You really love that club, don't you?"

"They're wonderful," I said. "Thanks for subbing for me again at the last second."

"I'm always happy to do it, Suzanne. Well, if you don't need me anymore, the dirty dishes are calling my name."

"That's disturbing on way too many levels," I said with a smile as I took back the front.

The rest of the morning was pretty calm, which was a welcome thing at that point. Several folks discussed Zane's murder in whispered tones, and one woman even pointed across the street to show another woman where the body had been found. For some reason, I kept expecting Tom to burst in with a handgun to take me hostage, no matter how irrational that might have seemed. I was jumpy, there was no doubt about it, which was probably a good thing, given the fact that we weren't much closer to catching the killer than we had been when I'd seen Zane's body pinned against the bench with that spear earlier.

After I eased my last few customers out the door at eleven sharp, I started working on our daily report and deposit while Emma took care of a lot of last-minute things like sweeping the front, cleaning the tables, and generally prepping us for shutting down for the day. When the reports all balanced out, I usually helped her, but on those dark days where we had discrepancies, I was useless to her.

Today everything worked out, though.

"How close are you to being finished?" I asked her as I wrote the last number on the day's deposit slip.

"I'm done," she said.

"Then you can go on home," I said as I tucked everything in the bank's deposit bag.

She lingered behind, though.

"Is something wrong?" I asked her.

"I don't know. It feels as though I'm missing something, you know?"

I grinned at her. "Could it be the three hours of doing our dishes before we opened for the day? Is there any chance that could be it?"

"You're probably right," Emma answered with a smile of her own. "I take it back. I don't think I could get used to working shorter hours. The day's just about perfect as it is now."

"I'm glad you feel that way," I said as I turned off the last light and led her out the door. After I locked up behind us, I said, "Have a good day."

"You, too," she said.

When I got to my Jeep, someone was waiting for me there, but this time, it was welcome.

"Hey, Grace," I said. "Did you finish your work early?"

"I did indeed."

"Where's your car?" I asked as I looked around.

"I decided to leave it at the library on the back lot and

walk over," she said. "There's no use advertising that we're together, is there?"

"You're getting trickier every day," I said as I let her in.

"I've got to admit that your warning about Tom has me spooked. Every time the library door opened, I nearly jumped out of my chair. I wish I had your nerve sometimes."

I laughed. "I've been jumpy all day myself. In fact, before Jake called me this morning, I was seeing bad guys lurking in every shadow."

"How's your state trooper doing?" Grace asked.

"Tired and frustrated at the moment, but he'll get his killer."

"You have a lot of faith in him, don't you?"

"Why shouldn't I?" I asked. "He's done it before, and there's no reason for me to believe that he won't do it again."

"Suzanne, why aren't you starting the Jeep?" Grace asked me as we just sat there.

"Where exactly should we go?" I asked her. "We've hounded our suspects repeatedly, and we've tracked down all the clues that we're probably going to find. What's left for us to do?"

"I say we go back to Union Square and talk to Janet and Billy again," she suggested. "Nobody knows where Tom is at the moment, and Candy's not going anywhere."

"Why not?" I asked her as I started the Jeep and drove toward Union Square.

"She has a business to run," Grace said. "She has to be there most of the time."

"No, I meant why not do as you just suggested and go back to Union Square?"

"Wow, that was easy."

"What can I say? It makes sense."

"I just hope that they are both still there," Grace said.

"They can't leave yet," I said. "There's an active police investigation going on."

"How long do you think they're going to hang around? I doubt that Chief Martin can make them stay."

"Why wouldn't Janet want to be here when her husband's killer is arrested?"

"Suzanne, you're assuming that she didn't do it herself."

"I'm not assuming that at all. I'm just saying that's how the police might perceive her absence before the case is solved."

"She might not care how it looks," Grace said. "After all, she wasn't shy about calling her insurance agent about Zane's policy."

"No, but we're not supposed to know that, remember? We only know because we broke into her hotel room."

"Nobody knows that we did that, though. As far as the rest of the world is concerned, Janet is just another grieving widow."

"Trust me, I'm sure she's just as high on Chief Martin's list of suspects as she is on ours."

"And we can't forget Billy," Grace said. "Did you see the way he looked at Janet yesterday at breakfast? That man clearly still has a crush on her."

"Maybe, but was it enough to make him kill his rival for her affections?" I asked.

"Nobody can really answer that but Billy."

"What about Tom?" I asked. "He wasn't high on my list until today, but I've got to tell you, he scared me in the park. I saw a side of him that I'd never seen before. Plus, he admitted taking the spear from the gym in the first place."

"Yes, but he claims that he dumped it outside," Grace said.

"That's not a bad cover story if he realized too late that he forgot to wipe his fingerprints off the murder weapon he used to kill Zane."

"Honestly, who would be that stupid?"

"Maybe drunk, not necessarily stupid, could explain it."

"I don't know," Grace said after a moment's hesitation. "I just can't see him as a killer."

I weighed my next words carefully. "Is that because of the facts, or from the history the two of you shared back in school?"

She didn't answer right away, and for a minute, I thought she was going to ignore the question completely. Finally, Grace said, "I truly don't know how to answer that."

I reached over and patted her arm. "It's hard to separate our personal feelings from our suspicions, isn't it?"

"It can be," she said. "That just leaves Candy. I wonder just how bad those pictures of her are? Would they be something she feels she needs to suppress, no matter what the cost?"

"She's not exactly shy about her clothing," I said. "If those pictures are enough to embarrass *her*, I'm guessing that they must be pretty bad."

"So her motive might be just as strong as anyone else's," Grace said. "We've got four viable suspects left, and no way to tell who really did it."

"That's why we keep pressing forward," I said as we came upon the Welcome to Union Square sign on the highway. "I don't want to announce our presence at the hotel, so let's park in the back lot and walk from there. How does that sound?"

"It's worth a shot," Grace said, and soon we pulled into the lot and parked with the employees of the hotel. My Jeep fit right in with the other vehicles parked there, and we set off for the main building on foot.

We never got there, though.

Two familiar voices were arguing in the garden that buffered the parking areas from the hotel, and if we were lucky, we just might be able to overhear what they were fighting about.

Chapter 16

"I don't care how you manage it! Just make it stop," Janet told Billy angrily in the garden. Grace and I hid behind an arbor covered with thick vines. It was dense enough to hide us both from view, but open enough to allow us to hear what they were saying.

"Janet, you're being unreasonable," Billy said calmly. "What makes you think that *I* have any control over what Suzanne and Grace do?"

"Figure it out, Billy. I can't afford to have anyone interfere with that insurance payment."

"Trust me; you've got more problems than that," Billy said. "You're more of a murder suspect than I am."

Grace must have shifted her weight at that point, because a stick snapped under her foot. In the quiet of the garden, the sound was loud and clear.

I quickly looked at Grace, who mouthed, "I'm sorry," but it was too late.

They'd heard us.

"What was that?" Janet said as she looked in our direction. "Hello. Is someone there?" she called out.

"Of course somebody's there," Billy said. "Can't you see them through the leaves? I'm taking off, Janet."

"You're not going anywhere," she snapped.

"You don't think so? Just watch me," Billy said as he hurried toward the hotel.

We weren't that lucky with Janet.

Instead of fleeing as well, she started walking straight toward us, and there was no way that we weren't about to be caught this time.

Chapter 17

"Are you two *spying* on me?" Janet said with indignation as she rounded the arbor and found us standing there.

"Of course not," Grace said.

"We *were* coming to *see* you, though," I added.

"So why didn't you announce yourselves when you first got here?" Janet asked us.

"We wanted to eavesdrop on you two a little first," Grace said brazenly.

Janet stared at us both for a full six seconds before she spoke again. "Well, I sincerely hope that you got what you wanted, because I'm finished talking to the both of you."

Janet turned back toward the hotel, but she'd only taken a few steps when I said, "You should know that we've discovered that you had a *pair* of motives for killing your husband."

She stopped in her tracks and whirled around to face us. "What are you talking about? Did you overhear something that you probably misunderstood, Suzanne?"

"Hardly. You wanted the money, but you also wanted Billy, didn't you?"

"Don't be ridiculous," she said. "Billy Briscoe and I were over a long time ago, and I'd rather have Zane back right now than all the money in the world. What makes you think otherwise?"

"We have sources that you don't even know about," Grace answered. "If all that you say is true, then why *exactly* did you want Billy to stop us from investigating your husband's murder?"

"Because I *need* that insurance money, and no amount of wishing is going to bring Zane back. I'm concerned that your snooping might interfere with my plan to collect what's coming to me and get out of this state forever. My late husband promised me riches beyond belief if I'd just be a little more patient, but I'd heard all of those promises before. It's a sad thing to admit, but in the end, he turned out to be worth more to me dead than he had ever been when he was alive."

"Where was he supposedly getting all of this money?" Grace asked her.

"If you must know, he was going to blackmail people that we knew," Janet said. "Is it any wonder that someone stabbed him with a spear? I warned him that he was playing a dangerous game, but he told me that he had it all under control. We can all see how well *that* worked out for him."

"You talk a good game, but you obviously care more about the money than you ever did for Zane. Isn't that true?" I asked.

"Once upon a time, back when I could trust him, I loved the man more than anything in the world. Then the lies started. Who knows? Maybe he'd been lying to me all along. I don't know. Anyway, he took whatever love I had for him and stomped on it with his boots. I shed a few tears for him when he died, but not many."

"It sounds as though you won't miss him at all."

"I can't honestly say one way or the other at this point, but I didn't kill him."

"Why should we believe you?" I asked her pointedly.

"I'll ask you another question. Why should *I* care what you believe, one way or the other?"

I was stumped to come up with an answer to that, but fortunately, Grace wasn't. "Because we have contacts everywhere, including with insurance agents who are eager for an excuse to delay benefit payments next to forever," she said.

I knew it was a bluff, and plainly Grace knew it as well. The question was, did Janet?

She tried to keep a brave face for as long as she could, but neither Grace nor I budged.

After a full thirty seconds, Janet sighed deeply, and then she said, "I give up. What do you want to know?"

"Who exactly was your husband blackmailing?" Grace asked her.

"I don't know. I have a few suspicions, but he never named names," Janet answered.

"Okay then, tell us who you *think* he might have been blackmailing," I said.

"For starters, he *definitely* had something on Candy Murphy. Tom Hancock has a secret that he's been hiding for years, and so does Billy. That's how I got him to help me."

"How did Billy help you?" I asked. I could see him killing Zane for Janet, or for the secrets that Zane held. Love for Janet was looking less and less like a factor in the murder.

"Do you want to know the truth? He didn't, not one single bit. The man was clearly drunk the night of the reunion, and when I had breakfast with him the next morning when you two showed up here, he was hung over like nobody's business. Billy Briscoe has been absolutely worthless to me from the start. I'd hoped to use his feelings for me to my benefit, but that didn't turn out to do me much good, either. He's been a complete wash."

Janet was a cold woman, icier than most I'd met in my life, but that still didn't make her a killer. "Janet, did you kill your husband, or did you have someone kill him for you?" I asked bluntly.

"No," she said flatly.

"Why should we believe you?"

"Do you mean my word isn't good enough?" Janet asked sarcastically.

"That's exactly what we mean," I said, deciding to

answer her anyway.

"I don't know how to prove to you that I didn't cajole or hire someone into killing my late husband. All I *can* do is show you that I didn't do it."

"How can you possibly do that?" I asked her.

"Because I wasn't even here," she said. "I got so mad at Zane for the way he behaved at the reunion that I drove straight home. I wasn't going to come back, but halfway there, I got pulled over for speeding in Charleston. It was one forty five AM, if you're interested. Anyway, I decided to come back after all. There was no telling what kind of trouble Zane might get himself into without me there to look out for him."

"Can you prove any of this?" Grace asked.

Janet reached into her purse and pulled out a slip of yellow paper. "Here's the ticket I got. I already showed it to Chief Martin."

"When did you do that?" I asked. I would have expected the chief to share something as important as that with me. I knew that I didn't have any rights to his information, but this was a courtesy I wanted from him.

"Ten minutes before you both got here. That's what prompted my fight with Billy."

So it appeared that Janet was off the hook, at least as far as committing the murder herself.

"What about that paper you dropped at the restaurant?" Grace asked.

"How did you find out about *that*?" Janet asked, and then she nodded before I had the chance to answer her. "The waitress at the restaurant told you, didn't she?"

"I won't answer that," I said. I was going to protect Maria and her family as much as I could.

"So it's okay to expect me to tell you everything, but you're not going to share anything with me. Is that it?"

"That pretty much sums it up," Grace said.

"Fine. Whatever. I found the slip of paper hidden in our hotel room. I asked Zane about it, but all he would say was that it was the key to our future. Do *you* two have any idea what those numbers mean, because it's been driving me crazy."

"We don't have a clue," I answered as Grace shook her head in agreement.

"Of course not. That would make my life too easy, wouldn't it? I know that those numbers were written in my husband's handwriting, and that they had something to do with this weekend, but that's all that I know. Zane always believed in keeping friends close, and enemies closer. I've got a hunch that philosophy is what ended up getting him killed." After a moment's pause, she asked, "Are we done here?"

I looked at Grace, who just shrugged.

"For now," I said.

"Forever," Janet replied, and then she stormed off back to the hotel.

"Should we follow her, or look for Billy?" I asked as a car sped out of the parking lot to the road.

Billy Briscoe was behind the wheel, and we were far enough from the Jeep that we'd never catch up with him.

"Well, there's no way that we're going to catch Billy in your Jeep, so we should probably talk to Candy again," Grace said with a wry grin.

"That sounds like a plan to me. I have a phone call to make first, though."

I dialed the chief's number, and he picked up on the first ring.

"I just talked to Janet Dunbar," I said.

Before I could get another word out, he said, "I was about to call you, Suzanne, but I had to confirm her story to make sure that it checked out."

"And did it?" I asked, feeling better about our situation.

"All across the board," he said. "She *couldn't* have killed Zane."

"Maybe not, but could she have hired someone to do it?"

"With what? They're not only flat broke, they're completely overextended. That was why I looked so hard at Janet. That insurance money will buy her out of most of her problems."

"She could have promised a payoff to the killer later," I said.

"That might work in the movies, but most paid killers demand something up front, and she just didn't have it. I'm sorry I didn't call you sooner, but like I said, I just found out."

"That's fine," I said. "There's more, though."

He was interrupted by someone just outside my hearing range, because when Chief Martin spoke again, he said, "I've got to go. We may have a lead about where Tom Hancock is hiding out. I'll talk to you later, Suzanne."

Then he hung up on me.

"You didn't tell him about Zane being a blackmailer," Grace said as I put my phone away.

"I never got the chance. He thinks they may have found Tom Hancock."

"Has the chief settled on him as the killer?" Grace asked me. "We have three suspects left ourselves. Does he know something that we don't?"

"If he does, he's not telling me," I said.

"So then we go talk to Candy," Grace answered.

"Since she's the only suspect left that we have any hope of finding, I think that's a fine idea."

As we drove back to April Springs, I wondered aloud about something. "Where do you suppose Candy got the money to open that gym of hers? Some of that equipment looked pretty expensive."

"I have no idea. I can't imagine someone giving her a bank loan for it, can you?"

"Hardly," I said. "What was she doing before she opened it? Maybe she saved her money and she's financing it herself. She told us that she had an investor, but that could have been a smokescreen."

"I heard that she was working at a hair salon in Hickory," Grace said. "I doubt that she made enough to pay for all of that."

"So someone probably is backing her," I said. "At least she didn't lie to us about that."

"It would appear so," Grace answered. "But how do we find out who her sugar daddy might be?"

"We could always just come out and ask her," I suggested.

"What makes you think that she'd tell us?"

"I don't," I said. "Still, there's *got* to be a way to find out. Who knows the ins and outs of business in April Springs better than anyone else? I'm talking about the behind-the-scenes scoop." I snapped my fingers and reached for my phone as I knew the answer was right in front of me.

"Who are you going to call?"

"Momma," I said.

When I got my mother on the phone, I asked her, "Do you happen to know how Candy Murphy is financing her new gym?"

"Suzanne, contrary to what you might think, I don't know *everything* that goes on in April Springs."

"But you can find out, can't you? I wouldn't ask if I didn't think it was important."

"Give me five minutes and I'll call you right back."

"She didn't know?" Grace asked me as I hung up.

"No, but she's going to poke around a little."

Two minutes later, my phone rang. "Hello?"

"Well, you're not going to believe this," Momma said.

"At this point, I'm willing to believe just about anything," I said.

"Leonard Branch is footing all of the bills for Candy's new venture."

"Mr. Branch?" I asked out loud. "You're kidding."

Leonard Branch was in his late fifties, a portly man who

owned a few small businesses around town. He was married to a woman who was unfortunately named Olive, a married name alone that should have kept her from tying the knot with him long ago. I couldn't imagine going through most of my life being married to that man and also bearing the burden of being known as Olive Branch. It was too much to ask of anyone.

"I only wish that I *were* kidding. The worst part of it is that Olive doesn't have a clue how Leonard is behaving."

"Are you telling me that there's more there than a business relationship between the two of them?" I asked. It was difficult imagining the sultry Candy with the heavyset Leonard under *any* circumstances.

"If my sources are to be believed, which I do, it's been going on for some time."

"Thanks for the information," I said, and then I added, "I think."

"Don't ask a question if you're not ready for the answer," she said happily, and then she hung up.

"Who would have ever believed it? Apparently Candy and Mr. Branch have been canoodling for some time. No wonder he financed her business venture."

"Canoodling?" Grace asked with a laugh. "Is that what the kids are calling it these days?"

"Call it what you will," I said. "I wonder if he's who Candy was trying to hide the pictures from? Could he withdraw his support if he knew they were out there?"

"He hardly has the right to take the high moral ground here, does he?"

"Given what he's been up to, I'm sure that he has no problem having double standards about anything," I said. "Now, how can we make this information work in our favor?"

"I'm not sure," Grace said. "I'll have to think about it."

I glanced at the clock on my dash. "Well, you've got five minutes until we get there. Think fast."

As I pulled up in front of the spa and gym, I asked Grace, "Have you come up with anything?"

"I've got nothing," she said. "How about you?"

"I guess we're going to have to just wing it," I said.

"Oh goody. I love it when we do that," she said as we both got out of my Jeep.

As we were walking toward the front door, I saw movement in a Cadillac in the parking lot. I couldn't believe it! Candy and Mr. Branch were actually making out in his car!

"I don't believe this," I said as I instantly changed directions.

Grace spotted it just after I did. "What are we going to do?"

"Just watch," I said as I approached the driver's side door. They still hadn't seen us, so I rapped loudly enough on the window to shake them both up. I didn't even feel guilty about doing it, even though I might have given Mr. Branch a heart attack.

They popped out of the car on either side, Candy smoothing her hair while Mr. Branch adjusted his loosened tie. "Suzanne, Grace, what are you two doing here?" she asked as nonchalantly as she could manage.

Before I could say a word, Grace answered, "Well, clearly we're not having as much fun as you two are."

"I don't know what you *thought* you saw, but we were just conferring about a business matter," Candy said sharply.

"Save it, Candy," I said. "We saw *exactly* what you were doing."

"I'm going to ask you this one more time. Why are you here?" Candy asked. Apparently Leonard Branch had been struck mute by our presence, because he couldn't manage a single word.

"We came to ask you if Zane was blackmailing you, and if you killed him because of it."

"You've lost your minds, the both of you," she said.

"*Nobody* was trying to blackmail me."

"That's where you're wrong," Mr. Branch finally said.

She whirled around to face him. "What are you talking about, Lenny?"

"Zane Dunbar came to see me four days ago. He had photographs of you he was threatening to release to the public if I didn't pay him off."

"Why would he come to *you*?" Candy asked.

"Clearly because *I'm* the one with the money," he answered. It was almost as though they'd both forgotten that we were even there.

"But how did he know about our … situation?"

"Do you honestly think it's *that* big a secret?" he asked.

"What did you do, Lenny?" Candy asked softly.

"Why, I bought them, of course," Mr. Branch answered. "What choice did I have? I couldn't let him hurt you."

"Mr. Branch, where were you the night of the murder?" I asked, suddenly realizing that he'd just supplied us with another, and quite unexpected, suspect.

"We were together," he said.

"You and Zane?" Grace asked him.

He shook his head. "No, Candy and me."

"Leonard Branch," Candy said with a warning tone in her voice. "You need to stay out of this."

"Why should I?" he asked. "*I'm* not ashamed of what we've been doing." He looked at me as he added, "Candy was with me that night. Olive was at her sister's, so Candy came over to my place. We're in love, and we're going to get married." The last bit he said with a shaky voice, as though he hadn't actually broached the subject with Candy yet. "Isn't that right, Candy?"

She looked at him in complete and utter shock. "*Married*? What gave you the impression that I'd *ever* marry you?"

"But you told me that you loved me," he said accusingly.

"I said a lot of things," Candy said icily.

"If you don't love me, then what has this all been about?"

"Don't play dumb with me," Candy said, the edge hard in her voice. "This was a business arrangement, plain and simple, and you knew it."

Mr. Branch couldn't have looked any more shocked if she'd shot him. Actually, that might have been kinder than the cutting words she'd just used on him.

"But I was going to leave Olive to be with you," he whined.

"I *never* asked you to do that," Candy said.

It finally sunk in that Leonard Branch had badly misinterpreted the situation. As he began to realize just where he stood, I could see his backbone stiffen. "I don't care what you thought. This was more than business to me."

"I'm sorry that I can't say the same thing," Candy said. As soon as she said it, it was clear by her expression that she knew that she'd finally stepped over the line. Getting a little closer to him, her voice softened as she said, "Forgive me, Lenny. I didn't mean it. I'm just distraught over all of this mess."

As she tried to put her arm in his, he jerked away as though she were on fire. "On the contrary, I have a feeling that was the first time that you've been honest with me since we met." He took a step away from her, and then he added, "You have thirty days to show a profit, or I'm withdrawing all of my funding."

"But I need more time," she said. Now Candy was the one who was pleading.

"Sorry, but that's all that I can spare. Now, if you ladies will excuse me, I've got some fences to mend with my wife. I just hope that she'll forgive my utter foolishness and stupidity."

"If you lead with that, you might just have a chance," Grace said to him.

"Then that's exactly what I'll do," he said as he got into his car and drove off.

"See what you did?" Candy asked as she looked murderously at Grace and me.

"*We* didn't do anything," I said. "You managed to do that all on your own."

She stared at us both for a moment more, and then Candy walked straight past us and into her gym. At least it was still hers for the next thirty days, anyway.

"I didn't mean for that to happen," I said, "but at least we finally got an alibi out of her."

"I'd say we got a lot more than that," Grace said. "And then there were two."

"The question is, which one is our killer: Tom Hancock or Billy Briscoe?"

"That's what we have to find out," Grace said. "I'm just not quite sure how we're going to go about it."

"We'd better come up with something soon," I said. "We're running out of time."

"Then I suggest that we get busy," Grace replied.

"I agree. The question is, what's our next move?"

We both spent a few moments thinking about it, and then finally Grace said, "Let's go back to Union Square."

"What is there left for us to do there? We've already eliminated Janet as a suspect, and Billy sure didn't look as though he was in any mood to talk to us anymore."

"That's a shame, then, because he's the last one left that we *can* talk to. I wonder where Tom is right now? Is the chief really hot on his tail? Do you think he's still around the county, or has he taken off for greener pastures?"

"If you ask me, I don't think he's gone far," I said.

"What do you base that on?"

"All I've got is intuition," I answered.

"Woman's?" Grace asked.

"No, investigative. I might be wrong, but what does it really matter at this point? We don't know where he is. If anybody catches him, it's going to have to be the police."

"So Billy it is," Grace said.

"Why not?" I asked as I started the Jeep and began to drive toward Union Square, and one of our last two suspects in the murder investigation of who really killed Zane Dunbar.

Chapter 18

On our way to Union Square, we drove past the high school gym where the reunion had been held. Out front, a teenaged boy struggled with a bike lock, evidently getting the combination wrong. We made eye contact as I drove past, and a look of pure frustration was clear on his face.

And that's when it hit me.

I pulled the Jeep into a nearby parking spot and shut off the engine.

"Why are we stopping here?" Grace asked me. "I thought we were going to go find Billy?"

"We were, but this might be even more important than that."

"What are we doing here, though? Helen and Henry have alibis, remember? They were getting married at the beach when Zane was murdered."

"Grace, this is something else entirely. I could be wrong, but we might have missed the biggest clue in the entire case."

"I'm listening."

As we got out of the Jeep, the teen finally freed his bike and rode away.

I just hoped that we had that much luck.

"What was the oddest prank played during the reunion?"

"Well, the cellophane was pretty gross," Grace said.

"I'm not talking about nasty."

"I don't know."

"The new locks," I said. "What if they weren't a prank at all, but a way of hiding evidence for blackmail nearby without raising suspicion?"

"Do you think Zane kept the info he was using at the school?" Grace asked.

"It's worth a shot," I said.

"What if we find the right locker? We don't have the combination."

"Maybe we do," I said. "Remember what Zane told Janet? That number was the key to their future."

Grace got it immediately. "3205. You think *that's* the key to getting the hidden information?"

"Why else would Zane have written those numbers down?" I asked. Steve, the white-haired janitor, was going out as we got to the door.

"What brings you two back here so soon?" he asked.

"We need your help," I said. "Have you done anything with those new locks you found on the empty lockers yet?"

"No," he said in disgust. "They are really heavy-duty. My bolt-cutters won't even work on them. I'm going to have to get a special blade for my saw and cut them off."

"That must make them pretty high-end," I said, beginning to feel better about my theory.

"It was an expensive prank, that's for sure," he said.

"Could we see the locks ourselves?" Grace asked him sweetly.

He shrugged. "I don't see why not. Come on. You can be my guests."

"That's nice of you," I said.

"Everybody's in an assembly, so the hallway should be empty," he said.

As Steve led us to the first locker, I entered the numbers Maria had reported seeing on the slip of paper Janet had dropped at Napoli's. Three to the left, past it again to the right for the twenty, and then straight to the five. If this was the right locker, we'd soon have the evidence that we'd been looking for.

It wouldn't budge.

"Try it again," Grace urged.

I did, twice more, with the same results.

"Where's the next one?" I asked.

"Right over here," he said. "Do you really think you can crack one of these? They're supposed to be foolproof."

"I'm not sure yet," I said as I worked on the second lock with the same end results.

"How about the next one?" I asked.

"It's over here," he said as he led the way. "If this doesn't work, there's only one lock left. How sure are you that you've got the right combination?"

"I'm not sure at all," I said. "All I can do is keep trying."

"I like your spirit, I'll say that much for you," he said.

The third lock refused to yield on my first attempt, and I thought about giving up, but I had to give it two more tries before I moved on to the last locker.

I couldn't believe it when the lock opened the next time I entered the combination!

"Well, well, well. That's impressive. What good does it do you, though?" Steve asked.

I didn't know, but whatever might be in there, I didn't want Steve to see it. "Grace, you were going to ask Steve something earlier, weren't you?"

She got it instantly. "Thanks for reminding me." She put her arm in the janitor's, and then she asked, "Steve, are you good with sticking doors?"

"I've managed to free one a time or two in the past," he said.

She led him away as she asked, "Could you give me a few tips, then?"

I doubted that he even knew what she was doing. I had to work quickly, though. I pulled the lock off the hasp and swung the locker open.

Inside were two envelopes.

One was marked with Tom Hancock's name, and the other had Billy Briscoe's on it.

Mr. Branch must have been telling the truth, because there wasn't an envelope for Candy Murphy there. He really had paid the blackmail money.

A sudden thought occurred to me as I stuck the envelopes in the back of my shirt. What had happened to the cash Zane had gotten? Had the killer taken it, or was it hidden somewhere else on the school grounds? I'd have to figure that out later. Right now, the most important thing for us to do was to find the murderer.

"It was empty," I said sadly as I rejoined Grace and Steve.

He shrugged. "Sorry about that," and then he turned back to Grace. "Like I said, I get off in an hour, and I'd be happy to come by your place and take a look at that door."

"If I can't fix it with your advice, I'll take you up on it later," she said as she disengaged her arm. "Thanks again for your time."

"It was my pleasure," he said.

We were three steps away when he called my name. Steve must have seen the bulge in the back of my shirt.

I was all set to explain when he asked, "Would you like that lock anyway? It might come in handy down the road."

"Sure, why not?" I asked as I took it from him and put it around a loop in my blue jeans.

"It wasn't *really* empty, was it?" Grace asked me once we were safely back outside.

"No, we hit pay dirt," I said as I pulled the envelopes out from the back of my shirt where I'd first tucked them.

"Suzanne, that was absolutely brilliant," she said as she looked at them.

"Don't give me too much credit. If we hadn't seen that guy struggling to open his bicycle lock, I *never* would have made the leap."

"You shouldn't sell yourself too short. If it hadn't been that, I'm sure that it would have been something else. I know you might not think this is ethical, but we need to read whatever is in those envelopes," she said as she tapped them in my hand.

"I couldn't agree with you more," I said.

"All right then," Grace answered with a grin. "As long as we're on the same page."

"I don't want to dig through this muck any more than you do, but it might be the only way we uncover the killer."

"Where should we go to look at what you found?" Grace asked.

"Let's head over to the donut shop," I said. "It's the only place we can be sure that no one is going to sneak up on us."

"That sounds like a good plan to me," she said.

We got to Donut Hearts, and after I let us in, I locked the door behind us.

"Should we sit here where it's comfy?" she asked as she pointed to my favorite couch.

"No, we're too exposed here," I said. "Let's do this in the kitchen. The barstools back there might not be as comfortable as the furniture out here, but at least no one will be able to see what we're up to."

"That's a good enough reason for me," she said.

Once we got in back, I flipped on some of the lights, not enough to shine through to the dining area, but enough to illuminate the pages that we were both about to read.

"Which one should we open first?" Grace asked after we were both settled in.

"Let's see what Tom's envelope says," I replied as I tore it open. Inside, there were IOUs, bank deposit slips, even larger ones for withdrawals, and a photocopy of a document that proved that Tom had stolen money from not only Zane, but a dozen other people as well.

"Do you know what this means?" I asked Grace as I pushed the documents across the counter toward her.

"Tom Hancock is a thief, pure and simple. What did he

do with all that money?"

"I don't know, but Zane had him dead to rights. If Tom didn't share some of it with Zane, he was going to jail."

"Man, and to think that I loved that guy once upon a time."

"Don't beat yourself up about it," I said. "You loved the boy, not the man that he became."

"In a way it's the same thing, isn't it?"

"Not on your life," I said. "We can't be responsible for who the people we once loved have become. Nobody has a crystal ball, Grace."

"Still, I shudder when I think about what might have happened this weekend if Zane hadn't been murdered."

"You can't live your life that way, either," I said. "Shall we see what he had on Billy?"

That envelope was more puzzling. It held an old clipping from a newspaper in Hickory dated the night before we all graduated from high school, with something attached to the back of it.

"It's a newspaper clipping?" Grace asked. "What's the story about?"

"A hit-and-run accident," I said. They hadn't caught the driver, and an older woman and her best friend had died at the scene.

"What's on the next page?" she asked me.

It was a picture of Billy on graduation day in his cap and gown. He was sporting a black eye, and he looked miserable.

Grace looked at it. "I remember that. Billy was so drunk he fell out of bed the day we graduated and gave himself a black eye. Remember?"

"I remember the story," I said. "But what if he made himself look the fool so no one would realize what had *really* happened?"

"Do you think that he killed those women back then?" Grace asked.

"Think about it. Did you ever see his car again after

that?"

"It's all coming back to me now," Grace said. "He had to ride to graduation with his parents because he said he'd left his car someplace with the keys in it and it had been stolen. I thought it was just one more stupid thing he'd done. I never dreamed that he was covering up a pair of murders."

"We need to call Chief Martin," I said as I pushed the papers aside.

"Suzanne, we still don't know which man is the murderer," Grace said.

"That may be, but if what's in Billy's envelope is true, he's *already* a killer."

I got the chief, and I was about to tell him what we knew when he cut me off. "I can't talk," he said in a near-whisper. "We're getting ready to take Tom Hancock down."

"Where are you?"

"Out at his parents' cabin on the lake," he whispered. "He doesn't even know that we're here."

"There's something else you need to know," I said.

"No time right now. We're getting ready to move," he said, and then he hung up on me.

"What just happened?" Grace asked.

"They're about to arrest Tom Hancock at his parents' lake house," I explained.

"Do they think he's the killer?"

"They must, but *I've* got a hunch that Billy did it," I said. "Tom might do some jail time for what he did, but Billy's crimes are a lot more serious, motive enough to kill Zane to protect himself."

"We don't know where Billy is, though," Grace said. "Do you think there's a chance that he's still at the hotel after what happened with Janet?"

"I don't know," I said, "but we have to look for him."

"I'm just as willing to run into a burning building as you are, but shouldn't we have some backup here,

Suzanne?"

"We can't call Jake, he's on that case all the way across the state, and George is visiting Polly in Raleigh. He's trying to woo her back here. I'm afraid that we're on our own, Grace, and we can't really wait around for reinforcements."

"Okay then," she said after taking a deep breath. "Let's go find Billy ourselves."

In the end, we didn't have to go as far as we'd feared we'd have to in order to track the man down, because he was waiting outside the donut shop for us both when we started to leave.

And what made matters worse was that there was a knife in his hand.

Chapter 19

"Get back inside," Billy ordered us as he jabbed the knife in our direction. It was no steak knife, either. It was some kind of large hunting knife, with razor-sharp edges that caught the sunlight. I shivered as I imagined what it would do to bare skin.

"Take it easy," I said, trying to calm him down a little.

He wasn't interested in that at all. "Suzanne, you have four seconds to get that door open," he said, "or one of you is going to get cut right here and now."

I fumbled as I tried to put the key in the lock, hearing an ominous countdown in my head as the seconds slipped past.

"Time's up," he said coldly just as the key made it in.

"I got it," I said as I pulled the door open.

"Get inside then," he ordered.

We did as he asked, and I prayed that someone had seen what had happened. It was broad daylight, and we were being abducted at knifepoint on Springs Drive! How had no one seen it happen? When I did something stupid or embarrassing in front of my donut shop, it seemed as though the entire town was watching, but now, when I needed them the most, they were nowhere to be found.

"What do you want from us?" Grace asked, her voice cracking a little as she spoke. I looked into her eyes and saw that she was petrified, more afraid than I'd ever seen her in my life.

"I'm not an idiot. If we stay out here, someone's going to see us," he said. "Get into the kitchen. Now!"

We did as he ordered, and as I walked into the tight room, I tried to think of something I could use as a weapon to fight back with. If he'd had a gun, our odds would have been quite a bit worse, but surely there was something back there I could use to fight him off.

Unfortunately, everything was put away. Emma had done too good a job cleaning up the kitchen, and the only thing close enough to grab was the heavy donut dropper I used to make our cake donuts. I knew from experience that if I could swing it hard enough, it would become a deadly weapon in its own right. There was a heavy indentation on the wall that proved that.

But how was I going to be able to get the time I needed to grab it and swing it at Billy's knife?

I'd just have to stall him until I could think of something.

"You didn't kill Zane so that you could have Janet for yourself, did you?" I asked him.

He shook his head and snarled. "Why would I want *her*? She was just one more way for me to get to Zane. *He's* the one who put it all together about what I'd done the night before we all graduated, and he claimed that he had substantial evidence on me. Where's that envelope?"

"What envelope?" I asked. I'd put it under the counter in the kitchen when we'd left, hoping that would be enough to keep it safe.

"Why do you think I'm here?" he asked. "I saw you leave the gym with two envelopes. It was pretty careless taking them out in plain sight like you did. Where were they hidden, anyway? I looked everywhere for them after I got rid of Zane."

Grace spoke up. "They were in one of the empty lockers at the school. Zane put new locks on four of them so he could hide the evidence in plain sight."

Billy nodded and even smiled a little. "That was crafty of him. How did *you* figure it out? I've been beating in my brains trying to find those papers."

"It took us awhile," I said.

"Let's see what we've got then," Billy said.

Once he had those papers, I knew that Grace and I were as good as dead. There'd be no reason for him to keep us alive once he had them, so I had to act before I turned them over to him. "I still can't believe that you killed Zane. You were drunk at the reunion. I know that firsthand. You approached me early on, remember, and you absolutely reeked of alcohol, Billy."

"I didn't take a single sip all night," he said. "I did, however, spill an entire drink on my clothes to make it appear that I was too drunk to kill Zane."

"So you'd been planning it all along," I said.

"Not really. I meant to get his hiding place out of him first, but he taunted me one too many times, so I stabbed him with that spear."

"Why did you use that as your murder weapon?" Grace asked him.

"I was outside waiting for Zane to leave when I saw Tom Hancock come out of the gym carrying it. When he threw it in the trash, I knew that it would make a perfect murder weapon. Better yet, it even had his fingerprints on it! I slipped on my gloves and grabbed it, but as I was hiding, Zane left the reunion and started off toward your donut shop. I couldn't exactly call out to him to get him to wait up, so I stalked him to the bench where he finally sat down. He laughed at me when I told him if he gave me the evidence he had on me, I'd let him live. I kind of lost my head, and before I realized what was happening, I stabbed him. I didn't mean to do it that hard, but it went right through him, and then he was dead. I was hoping that he had the evidence against me on him, but all I found was a lot of cash. Evidently *somebody* decided to pay him off." He frowned at that, and then Billy said, "Enough talking. Let's have that envelope. And don't try to tell me it's not here, because I saw you with it earlier."

It was time to act. Instead of walking to the shelf where the envelopes were, I headed toward the heavy donut dropper instead.

Grace must have realized what I was doing, because

just as I reached it, she shouted, "Look out!"

Billy stared at her as though she'd lost her mind, and I grabbed the steel dropper. It was heavy in my hands, but I swung it with all my might.

I wanted to break his arm with it.

Billy turned in time to stop me from doing that, but the knife did go flying out of his hand when I made contact.

I started to swing at him again, but I couldn't manage it before he attacked me.

Billy had me pinned against the wall, and I could see the rage filling his eyes. Using his forearm, he pressed it harder and harder against my throat, and I felt my head begin to spin.

The dropper fell from my hand as I fought with everything I had to keep him from choking the life out of me.

And then I heard the sound of an impact, and just as suddenly as the killing pressure had started, his hands fell away from me and he dropped silently to the floor.

I tried to catch my breath as I looked over at Grace, who still held the donut dropper in her hand. There were bits of blood and hair on one edge of it, and I wondered if Billy Briscoe was dead.

"You're right, Suzanne," she said. "That thing weighs a ton."

"Thanks for saving me," I said in a choked whisper.

"I'm the one who should be thanking you. If you hadn't attacked him, we *both* would have been dead," Grace said as she pulled out her cellphone.

"Is he dead?" I asked as I nudged Billy with my foot.

Grace knelt down for a moment, and then she stood up as she said, "He's still breathing."

"Call the chief," I said as I stumbled to one of the stools in the kitchen.

"In a second," Grace said as she pushed the knife well out of his reach. Then she handed the dropper to me and added, "Just in case he gets up."

"I don't think he'll be getting up for quite awhile," I said.

Still, I was relieved when we heard the first police siren, and I had recovered enough from the attack to let the chief in when he came to the door.

"Tom didn't kill Zane," he said after I opened the door.

"No, but he's a bad guy, too. We've got evidence on him and Billy both in the kitchen."

"Is Billy still out cold?" he asked.

"No, he's awake, but he keeps complaining about having a splitting headache," I said with a grin. "Grace clocked him pretty good."

"I'm just glad that you two are all right," the chief said as more officers came in.

"I'm going to be hoarse for a little bit, but all in all, we're both just dandy," I said.

My cellphone rang at that moment, and I saw that it was Jake.

"How did you know?" I asked before I even thought about it.

"How did I know what?" he asked. "I just wanted to tell you that we caught our killer."

"That's brilliant," I said.

"Suzanne, what's wrong with your voice?"

I knew there was no way I'd be able to lie to him about what had happened. After I brought him up to speed, I finished by saying, "There's no need to hurry back. Everything's fine here. How did you catch your killer, anyway?"

"It disgusts me to admit it, but it was pure dumb luck. The man was driving without his seatbelt, and a cop pulled him over when he spotted it. He had a bloody knife poking out from under his seat, and we were able to identify it as the murder weapon."

"Hey, as long as he's in jail, right?"

"I guess so, but I still would have liked to have caught him myself," Jake said. "Anyway, there's nothing left for me to do here. I'm heading your way, so expect me in four hours."

"But you're six hours away from April Springs," I said.

"Sure I am, if I don't have lights and a siren at my disposal," Jake replied. "I'm glad that you two are okay."

"So am I," I said. "Drive safely."

"Suzanne, I can be quick or I can be safe, but I can't be both," he said, a little of the good humor coming back into his voice.

"I can wait a little bit longer, then. I choose safe."

"Spoilsport," he said with a laugh, and then he hung up.

After Billy was in custody, Grace and I stayed behind at the donut shop for a minute. We'd have to go to Chief Martin's office to make our statements, but he was letting us come in my Jeep. The police chief had already gathered up the knife and the blackmail evidence, so the donut shop looked to be in perfect order again.

As we walked outside and I locked the place up, Grace said, "Well, I've made up my mind."

"About what?" I asked.

"I'm going to make full restitution for what I stole," she said.

"Grace, it was a long time ago. Besides, there's nobody left in the Dunbar family to give the money to, unless you're thinking about giving it to Janet."

"That wasn't exactly what I had in mind," she said.

"Then what are you going to do?"

"I'm donating five thousand dollars to the April Springs High School scholarship fund in the name of the Dunbars," she said.

"But what you stole wasn't nearly that valuable," I said. I knew that kind of money would be a real stretch for her to give up, despite her nice annual salary.

"It's what it's going to take to make me feel better," Grace said. "Do you think the Dunbars would have approved?"

"I think it's a smashing idea," I said. "I'd match it if I could, but unfortunately, that would wipe out my entire nest egg."

"That's okay. It's the thought that counts," Grace said with tears in her eyes.

"I might not be able to manage as much as you can, but I can at least add fifty bucks to the pot," I said, though even that would be a stretch at the moment.

"You don't have to do that," Grace said. "After all, it was *my* crime."

"I understand that, but it's my way to show my support. What do you say?"

"Thank you, Suzanne. I don't know what I'd do without you."

"Let's hope that you never have to find out," I said as I hugged her before we got into my Jeep.

As we drove to the chief's office, I thought about what secrets could do, and how they could fester over the years until they took hold of us. No good had come from Zane Dunbar's attempts to cash in on people's past mistakes, and he'd even died for trying.

In the end, Candy had lost her spa and her financial backer, Tom and Billy were both going to jail, and Zane was dead.

It made me happy that I was a simple donutmaker, and that all of my past sins were known to the world. I hadn't been an angel, but at least I'd managed to put my past behind me and move forward.

And the life I had now was better than any I ever could have imagined in high school.

I wouldn't have gone back and lived it all over again for all of the money in the world.

RECIPES

The Best Chocolate Cake Donut Recipe I've Ever Made!

I've been making donuts for many years, but I can say without a doubt that for me, this is the best chocolate cake donut recipe I've ever come up with. These donuts are dense, rich, and downright decadent! They are as tasty as they are pretty, and that's saying something. An added bonus is the way your kitchen smells as these are baking, almost enough to satisfy your sweet tooth by itself! We've topped these donuts with chocolate glazes and icings in the past, but our favorite way to eat them now is to dust powdered confectioners' sugar on top of them. Like snowy peaks on dark mountains, they are quite lovely to look at all on their own. Add the richness of the donut itself and they are ambrosia. We've added semi-sweet chocolate chips into the batter on occasion in the past as well, and you can't go wrong trying it yourself, but in the end, this simple yet elegant recipe needs no other additions or improvements.

INGREDIENTS

Dry
1 cup flour, unbleached all purpose
1/3 cup unsweetened cocoa powder
1 teaspoon baking soda
1/4 teaspoon salt

Wet
3/4 cup half and half (whole milk, 2 percent, or even 1 percent can be substituted)
1 egg, beaten
2/3 cup brown sugar (dark for more flavor, light for less)

4 tablespoons unsalted butter, melted
2 teaspoons vanilla extract
1/2 vanilla bean seeds, scraped

Topping
powdered confectioners' sugar, as needed for dusting
the finished donuts

INSTRUCTIONS

In a medium-sized bowl, mix the flour, cocoa powder,
baking soda and salt together until blended. In another
bowl, mix the half and half, egg, brown sugar, butter,
vanilla extract and vanilla beans together. Pour the wet
ingredients into the dry, stirring until they are
incorporated together.

Bake in a 375 degree F oven or in your donut maker for
5-8 minutes, then remove to a cooling rack and dust
immediately with powdered confectioners' sugar.

Yields 10–12 donuts.

Baked Lemon Magic Donuts

Sometimes nothing will satisfy my sweet tooth like lemon flavoring, and when I'm in one of those moods, I turn to these donuts to feed my craving. These donuts look lovely when they are finished, and they present a delicately light touch when a heavier donut just won't do. They are particularly good with the lemon glaze recipe added on the next page. Don't be afraid to try these, but make sure you're a fan of lemon flavor first. They aren't for the unsure or the undecided.

INGREDIENTS

1 cup readymade pancake mix (we use Bisquick, but any mix will do)
1/2 cup half and half (whole milk, 2 percent, or even 1 percent can be substituted)
2 tablespoons unsalted butter, melted
2 tablespoons granulated sugar
1 tablespoon lemon juice
2 teaspoons lemon zest
1 teaspoon vanilla extract (lemon extract could be substituted)
1/2 vanilla bean, scraped

INSTRUCTIONS

In a bowl, mix all of the wet ingredients together, reserving the pancake mix for last. Once the wet ingredients are incorporated, add the mix and blend until combined, being careful not to over-mix, as this could cause denser donuts.

Bake in a 375 degree F oven or in your donut maker for 5-8 minutes, then remove to a cooling rack and dust immediately with powdered confectioners' sugar or the glaze from the next page.

Yields 10-12 donuts.

Lemon Glaze For Any Donut
(but particularly good for the Baked Lemon Magic Donut recipe above)

As promised, here's the super simple lemon glaze for donuts. It couldn't be easier.

INGREDIENTS

1/4 cup powdered confectioners' sugar
1 teaspoon milk (2 % or 1 %)
1 teaspoon lemon juice

INSTRUCTIONS

Combine all ingredients in a small bowl and whisk until combined. Drizzle this mixture on top of any donut and enjoy!

Vanilla Goodness Donuts

I have a confession to make. Vanilla is one of my favorite flavors in the world, especially when real vanilla beans are added into the mix. There's something about the richness of the tang of vanilla that makes my taste buds zing. Now don't get me wrong; I'm a huge fan of chocolate as well. There are just times when vanilla is what I'm looking for, a lighter taste to complement the heavier flavors I encounter most days in my baking. I should admit from the start that these donuts aren't the prettiest ones you'll ever make. They are dense, thick-bodied, and have a homemade look to them, but the vanilla flavoring is worth forgiving them their rather dowdy appearances, at least in my opinion.

INGREDIENTS

Dry
1 cup flour, unbleached all purpose
1 teaspoon, baking powder
1/8 teaspoon nutmeg (fresh is best, but store-bought is good, too)
1 dash salt

Wet
1/2 cup half and half (whole milk, 2 percent, or even 1 percent can be substituted)
1/4 cup granulated sugar
4 tablespoons unsalted butter, melted
1 tablespoon honey
1 egg, beaten
2 teaspoons vanilla extract
1/2 vanilla bean, scraped

INSTRUCTIONS

In a bowl, mix the flour, baking powder, nutmeg and salt until incorporated. In another bowl, mix the half and half, sugar, butter, honey, egg, vanilla extract and vanilla bean seeds together. Mix and blend the dry ingredients into the wet until they are combined, being careful not to over-mix, as this could cause denser donuts.

Bake in a 375 degree F oven or in your donut maker for 6-8 minutes, then remove to a cooling rack and dust immediately with powdered confectioners' sugar or unsweetened cocoa powder.

Yields 10-12 donuts.

If you enjoy Jessica Beck Mysteries and you would like to be notified when the next book is being released, please send your email address to newreleases@jessicabeckmysteries.net. Your email address will not be shared, sold, bartered, traded, broadcast, or disclosed in any way. There will be no spam from us, just a friendly reminder when the latest book is being released.

Also, be sure to visit our website at jessicabeckmysteries.net for valuable information about Jessica's books.

Made in the USA
Lexington, KY
24 February 2014